Heaven's Thief

ERICA M NICKELS

Printed in the United States of America

First Printing, 2020

ISBN: 9798687056922

For information about purchasing and permissions contact Erica M Nickels at erica.m.nickels@gmail.com

www.ericamnickels.com

Cover design by Erica Nickels. Cover photo by Amariei Mihai on Unsplash

This is a work of fiction. Names, characters, places, and incidents either are products of the author's imagination or are used fictitiously. Any resemblance to actual persons, living or dead, events, or locales is entirely coincidental.

Scripture quotations are taken from THE HOLY BIBLE, NEW INTERNATIONAL VERSION®, NIV® Copyright © 1973, 1978, 1984, 2011 by Biblica, Inc.™ Used by permission. All rights reserved worldwide.

For mom: because this is your favorite story I've written to date. Thank you for raising me in the love of Christ.

But store up for yourselves treasures in heaven, where moths and vermin do not destroy, and where thieves do not break in and steal.

Matthew 6:20 NIV

Part 1

I

ONE

With downcast eyes, One tucked the folded piece of cloth away for safekeeping. The rain dripping from the gray sky chased the treasure One had stolen from it. He had risked his life for the cloth and the rain was just another kick in the shins he didn't need after the day's failure. The scrap in the pocket of One's black jeans looked like little more than a dishrag, but it was a piece of the original Torn Curtain, split down the center as Christ's life was given in sacrifice[1] to make the whole Earth righteous. That was little more than a sick joke if One had anything to say about it. Heaven appeared to have turned a blind eye on the everyday happenings where demons held dominion.

Ironically, the fragment of curtain wasting space in One's pocket was as close as it had been in millennia to the most effective weapon One owned: one of the nails that had held Christ to the cross.[2] The two artifacts had been scattered across the world, both relics of a holier time in human history, now both held by heaven's enemy.

One ducked into his destination, the closest bar to the train station he'd just left, hours of lonely travel dragging behind him like a ship's wake. If One were human, the bartender might have asked for ID from the teenager walking in at 1 am, but even the best bouncers tended to overlook One. It was all part of the charm.

"Something hard, thanks." One slid onto a stool, making brief eye contact with the bartender.

The man tipped his head in One's direction, moving around behind the counter to fill the order. According to movies, the gentle old man should serve the drink and rest his elbow on the counter across from One, not much else to do so late at night when business was slow. He would smile with eyes that had seen things and ears that had heard a hundred stories, then he would ask One what problem required such a strong solution.

But no bartender, nor waiter, nor service worker had ever asked One anything. They all saw right past One like he existed on a different plane of reality. If anyone asked this bartender about the person of unclear age with a shock of messy white hair and dark blue eyes that crackled like cold water in a flash freeze who had downed five shots of 150 proof liquor and started a fight, he would laugh and say he'd definitely remember someone like that. He might claim he wouldn't let someone have that much to drink. And yet, the bartender set the shot glass on the shiny countertop in front of One without a second glance. Nobody would be asking anything about One anyway so there was no need to remember.

With practiced, steady hands, One dipped a hand into the pocket of his white puff vest, sodden and notably heavy from the downpour outside. He extracted a small glass vial of black liquid and turned the shot dark with a single drop, tipping his head back to let it all run down his throat at once.

As expected, it was nasty. One raised his hand at the bartender for another shot, something to wash down the foul taste of demon blood, barely tolerable even with alcohol. The liquor on its own wasn't bad. One motioned for a third shot.

By this point, the bartender would have to question any normal customer about the heavy drinking. But One wallowed alone in self-pity that more than justified the need to lose all inhibition. The vial of demon blood kept snug in his pocket was the last he had. It wouldn't last long. One would slowly and painfully die without the poison that kept him alive.

The fourth and fifth shots disappeared in a deepening haze. One's blood alcohol content would be dangerous by human standards but by his own limits, not enough to shed the weight of the day's hollow disappointment.

Two men occupied another table a short distance away, the only other customers in the open-late bar an hour before it closed. Foam still streaking the sides, they each had an empty glass of beer in front of them. Several more muddled the last few hours. Their voices had risen to low shouts of disagreement and they ignored the warning from the bartender to quiet down. They were fighting over something as inconsequential as a woman. It wasn't worth getting upset over, but the yelling was starting to make One's head hurt. The bad day paired with too much alcohol left him volatile.

One slid off the barstool and approached the loud table. He ran a hand through his white hair, pushing it back from blurry eyes and glared at the two men. "Hey. Your catfight is getting loud and some of us are trying to unwind here. Do us all a favor and shut it."

The shorter of the two men stood in a hurry, swaying as he did. His glare was unfocused and his eyes never met One's. "Listen! You have no business interfering in our conversation! Go home if you want to drink alone!"

"Siddown…" The second man's voice slurred worse than the first but his gaze was steadier as he glared at One, hesitating only at the sight of the raised, white scar under One's eye. "If y'know what's good for ya, you'll leave us 'lone."

"What's good for me?" One crossed his arms. "You don't know a thing about what's good for me. Get out of my face."

"Out of your face!? You get out of *my* face!" The first man was at it again, stumbling toward One.

In a flash of annoyance, One slipped a hand into his pocket to pull out the crucifix nail. The tool didn't appear sharp or dangerous, large enough to be a railroad stake but weathered by millennia of traveling the Earth, passing from hand to hand until it landed in One's, but it packed its own punch. When the man got too close for comfort, One pulled the point of the nail across the man's forearm, pulling blood to the surface.

He yanked his arm back, eyes widening as he clasped his other hand over the injury. "Hey! You cut me! What was that for?"

The second man rounded on One, fists raised. "What are you trying to pull here, pal?"

One ducked the punch and delivered one of his own. He stepped out of the way as the man wobbled to the floor. One spat in his general direction and headed for the door of the bar, done drinking for the night.

The bartender ran over to help his patrons, but there wasn't much to do. The man One had cut would never fully heal. The gash in his arm would stop bleeding in time, but it would never fade away, open and ragged for the rest of his life. And he was lucky. The holy nail dealt a lot more damage to the immortal than it could inflict on the mortal.

Reminded of the celestial nuisance that was the half-empty vial of demon blood, One darted from the bar. No one bothered to come after him and no one would be able to place the cause of the disturbance if questioned about it.

All part of the charm.

Stepping out onto the street again, the air was frigid cold to One and he pulled the sleeves of his black turtleneck down over his hands. The rain had reduced itself to a light drizzle, but misery still infected the forecast. With the crucifix nail tucked away in the pocket of his black jeans next to the torn curtain, One ventured down the dark street, turned a corner, and vanished.

II

CASEY

Putting on a burst of speed, Casey Wickstrom crossed the finish line ten strides ahead of anyone else. She slowed her pace to the sound of cheers, a faint grin creeping onto her face as she jogged to a stop, hands behind her head to catch her breath. From the instant she'd stepped into the stadium, she had dominated the track meet, surprising no one.

A blonde girl a few inches shorter and a few seconds slower crossed the finish line in third place. She approached her best friend, tugging on her dark, curly ponytail. "Nice one, Casey."

Casey returned the gesture, replying in between gasps for air. "Not so bad yourself, Rose. With the seniors already graduated, there's no doubt the day belongs to the juniors once again."

Glancing at the remaining runners flailing across the finish line and those standing on the sideline, Rose shrugged. "The day belongs to you. The junior class is fast, but you're the one with the medals."

The sun dipped behind the bleachers and the spectators shifted on the metal benches, anticipating the final awards ceremony and the end of the track meet. The high school athletes congratulated each other before the loudspeaker congregated them in a line in front of the stands. Casey hid herself in the middle with the other juniors, humble curiosity on her face like she didn't know for certain already she would be called to step out of line for more awards than anyone else.

By the time awards had been given out, the late afternoon sun wasn't as effective in drying sweat from the athletes' bodies, but Casey enjoyed the cool June evening for what it brought. Three medals hung on ribbons around her neck, cold against her chest, and she clutched a trophy in one hand, naming her top performer at the women's track meet. Casey shook the hand of her coach as she received the trophy and stepped forward to take the microphone though it wasn't offered to her.

"Thank you," Casey said into the mic flashing a brilliant smile to the crowd. "Thank you for another great year of track. It's crazy to think I'll be a senior when school starts up again, but I think I speak for everyone in my class when I say we well deserve this place at the top of the food chain. I'd like to personally thank my family for their support, Jesus Christ for blessing me, and all the athletic staff at school for giving me this opportunity."

"Alright, Casey, we don't need an acceptance speech." The coach smirked, recapturing the mic. "Thank you to all the parents for coming today to watch your students. It's been a pleasure to work with them as usual and I'll see everyone here again when school starts."

The crowd dispersed quickly after that, the high schoolers all exchanging hugs since this would be the last track practice before summer break, meaning months before some of them would see each other again. Casey milled around with Rose, savoring the sound of her medals clinking together until it was time to pack up and leave.

Rose pulled on a jacket with West High School's name and logo across the back, slinging a backpack on, eyeing Casey's absent stare at the horizon. "Are we all going out again tonight?"

"Of course." Casey's eyes were closed, her arms outstretched, letting the summer night caress her exposed skin. She waited to move until Rose sighed and grabbed the strap of the bag on her own shoulder, pulling her toward the stairs out of the stadium.

As with every meet, Casey left her heart on the track when she left. She'd find it again bright and early the next morning when she set off for a run around the neighborhood on her own. You can take the girl away from the track, but you can't take track away from the girl. But for tonight, there was a party to be had and Casey needed to get home to shower before going out again. As the top track and field athlete of the junior-turning-senior class, she held the moral obligation to look spectacular, which she always did.

A boy several inches taller than Casey ran up beside her, touching his hand to the small of her back but removing it again after contacting the sweat-damp material. "Nice running, babe."

Casey smiled and swayed in the direction of her boyfriend, careful not to touch him and get sweat on him or his letterman jacket that he held over his shoulder. There was no chance he'd need it in June, but he carried it around for the same reason Casey refused to take the medals from around her neck even though the clinking was beginning to annoy her. "Thanks for coming, Dylan. Want to come with the rest of us out for dinner?"

"It's not going to be fine dining or anything; I hope you're okay with that." Rose leaned around Casey to raise one eyebrow at Dylan.

Snickering, Dylan placed his free hand in the pocket of his shorts. "You can stop teasing me about that. I'm coming with no matter where you guys go."

Rose shrugged. "I'm just saying, I don't know what kind of vegan options McDonald's is going to have under 500 calories."

Casey jumped to the defense of her boyfriend's offended expression. "We're not going to McDonald's. Dylan, you can follow me home in your car and then we'll go together to dinner after I shower. Rose, I'll see you there."

The blonde girl saluted and broke off from the couple in the school parking lot and headed for her car as Casey scoured the lot for her mother, knowing Dylan wouldn't like her riding in his car while she was sweaty.

"Hey, Casey," Dylan nudged her arm before she left too, "That was a cute speech you gave down there at the end. I didn't know you were Christian."

Casey smirked. "It's just what you say in speeches after you kick some butt."

"So you're not Christian?"

"I mean, sort of." Casey spied her mother's car and took a few steps in that direction. "We don't really go to church anymore, but we used to when I was a kid. It's not that important to me anymore.[3] Why? Are you religious?"

Dylan shook his head. "Nah. I was just curious. I'll see you at your house. We... we're not actually going to McDonald's are we?"

Casey laughed. "No, we're not. It's the end of the track season; we're going somewhere nicer than that. I'll make sure it's somewhere with good vegan options for you. Don't take Rose seriously. She's messing with you."

"Alright." Dylan took a step back and waved. "Godspeed, religion girl."

Laughing, Casey skipped away.

III

ONE

As many times as he'd done it before, contacting demons still made One's head hurt and muscles clench with effort to maintain the link. Eyes shut tight, One could still feel the dust storm swirling around him in the blackness, forming images that shifted and broke away just as quickly. Looking down his nose at One, the face of the demon held the shape of the dust fluidly, particles completing the image as quickly as they flew around the space.

"Gogmuth," One gasped the demon's name, feeling power ripple through the air. One had never called upon this particular demon before, but it was a safe bet that he liked hearing the sound of his name. It made demons feel important, feared, respected. It also showed that One wasn't inexperienced or too scared to make a deal. Demons didn't like wasting their time with humans and paramortals who didn't know what they were doing.

The demon smirked as it watched One, sizing up its next

employee. It had prolonged the contact already without saying anything, just watching One struggle, forcing him to maintain the link between worlds to communicate, a test of strength. "You're very good at hiding, aren't you," Gogmuth mused. "For someone with your accomplishments, you stay out of trouble pretty well. For someone with your *failures*, it's impressive you're still alive. And you don't let your past get in the way. Good work."

"It doesn't matter." One gritted his teeth against the sardonic tone, wondering how long this demon was going to make small talk. "All that matters is who I am now and what I can steal for you."

"Yes, I see that," Gogmuth murmured, perusing One's personal history like a resume.

It hurt, letting the demon inside his mind. There was no way to restrict access, no way to close doors off the main hall now that One had opened the front door and invited Gogmuth inside.[4] He couldn't intervene as the presence tore from room to room, checking shelves, opening closets, looking through every memory, fact, and facet of One, whether or not it was information he wanted to share.

"Very impressive." The demon let the job interview continue, prying into one of the most painful memories One held, simultaneously, proof of one of his greatest accomplishments. "I didn't think I'd ever have the pleasure to meet a member of the crew who stole the Ark of the

Covenant."

One didn't reply. Gogmuth didn't need to know any more about the Ark. It wasn't relevant and all the information was in One's head if the demon really wanted to know the whole story. The dust creature was still making conversation while it waited to see if One's concentration would break and the connection would flicker out.

Gogmuth laughed, making the dust forming his image fly faster through the air. "Bit of a sore spot there I see. We don't have to talk about that if you're still hurt."

"I have something to offer you," One spoke up, ignoring the taunts.

"Something to offer me? Even though I'm the one with the job for you? I'm delighted; tell me more." Mocking interest laced the demon's tone.

If One could've rolled his eyes through all the sand and dust whipping around, he would've. He reached into the pocket of his jeans. The missing presence of the crucifix nail didn't provide One with any comfort, but demons were very good about checking pockets for weapons, especially immortal weapons, so One had to leave it outside the line. He drew out the folded cloth instead, holding tight so it wouldn't be swept away by the flying sand. "Part of the original torn curtain," One announced. "I picked it up along the way on my last bounty. Thought it might be of some value."

"But your client didn't want it," Gogmuth finished the

statement, sounding increasingly amused.

In the presence of certain demons, One might have beefed up the desirability of the object, but he figured there wasn't much sense constructing lies in this case. The demon probably already knew the whole story anyway, based on the speed he was tearing through One's mind, leaving no stone unturned. "No," One kept his eyes on the demon, warning it against any trickery, "they didn't want it. Like I said, I picked it up on the way. It wasn't part of our contract. But if an angel touched this, it would be way more valuable than most celestial relics. Even if you don't have a use for it, I'm sure you could make something if you found another demon who did—"

"Silence," Gogmuth said in a soft whisper as a flurry of dust choked off One's words and made his eyes water. He was having fun and could probably play this game all day. "Am I some minor devil in the market for angel relics?"

One ducked his head in humble submission. "No, but I'll sell it to you cheap as a bonus for picking up your job."

Gogmuth laughed again, intensifying the sandstorm. By this point, the unholy creature had ripped its way through the whole of One's mind and there was nothing more to explain aloud. The demon knew that One was a reliable thief of angelic artifacts but stuck to petty trinket robberies: angel wing feathers and trumpets and the occasional halo if the price was right. He didn't often stray into the darker side of demon business. But Gogmuth also knew by now that work had been hard to come by lately and One was nearing the end of his emergency stash of demon blood. "And that's why you answered my call," Gogmuth mused aloud. "It's been a long time since you've been involved in soul trade, One. Are you sure you're up for it?"

"I'm fully capable of bringing your target in," One grunted, slipping the cloth back into his pocket. Mentioning it again would likely bring consequences.

More difficult than petty robbery but much more rewarding was the bounty placed on the capture of human souls. It was dirty work with many more risks, but One was desperate. If he couldn't get his hands on some demon blood soon, his life would fade; mortal blood alone in his veins was not enough to sustain him.

The wind and flying dust subsided slightly so the demon's face was clearer to see. "I think the deal is sealed then."

"I want to be paid up front," One interjected, a gutsy request to ask of a demon with even half Gogmuth's strength.

The creature only laughed, its face of dust flaking and chipping away to nothing. "Nice try. If you weren't such a good thief, I might've considered."

Sand poured from One's eyes as they flew open. He coughed more dust out of his lungs, cursing the demon for its dramatic flair. Hands scrabbling against the hard floor, One collapsed from the kneeling position and grabbed the crucifix nail left outside the outer edge of the pentagram. The danger was gone now that the link was broken, but the weapon still brought familiar comfort, clutched in One's hand.

In the center of the star shape on the basement floor, One sat up, groaning. He felt like he'd taken a ride in a clothes dryer on a roller coaster, not to mention the sand scratching at his eyes and throat with every blink and breath. His head pounded from Gogmuth's field day inside of it and the file of information left behind, instructions for the soul One had been hired to capture.

One would clean up first to get rid of all the sand the impudent demon had sent back to his realm, then take a nap to clear the throbbing headache and lingering drunkenness. Then, he would be ready to head back out and rejoin the soul trade.[5]

It was important to start hunting immediately after contacting Gogmuth, but One barely made it up the stairs from the basement before collapsing on a couch, passed out. When he woke up again, gold coins and jewelry lay scattered on the floor instead of squirreled away on shelves. It looked like an earthquake had hit. One frowned, but stood up, stepping over the misplaced trinkets.

The house was stiflingly warm and One had discarded his black turtleneck sometime during the nap. He picked it up from the floor, shaking off a few more gilded knickknacks.

One rubbed his eyes, aware of a hot pain in his back. The house had been harder to navigate lately, but he found a mirror and twisted to look over his shoulder. Centered on his lower back was what appeared to be a large tattoo, though it was much more than a decoration. It was an anti-possession rune, warding away any demon that tried to make its home in One's body.[6] Anyone who worked regularly with demonic presences had one. Those foolish enough to think they didn't need a rune were possessed before they had a chance to regret it.

Within a pentagram, a person opened a communication link to the demon realm, miles beneath the earth's surface and unreachable by natural means. By staying within the design's outer circle, both parties were safe from any physical harm from the other; no weapon could pierce skin, stop heart, or take life. That didn't mean demons were reckless in who they allowed contact with. If One brought the crucifix nail into the pentagram, all he would have to do was step through the link. He would find himself in the demon's realm, blade at the ready. Connections were usually peaceful though, so there was no reason for One to bring a weapon as long as his anti-possession rune kept him safe from demonic attack.

The rune on One's back throbbed with heat straight from hell, a warning indicating that Gogmuth had tried his very best to slip inside One's body as he had with his mind. One sighed, pulling the shirt back on. This would be the last time he ever agreed to work a soul trade job. The demons that commissioned for humans were much more powerful and dangerous. They challenged runes and never played by the rules.

One was well aware of the other present the demon had left him. The information on the targeted soul had been copied into One's mind. He read just far enough into it to pick up the name and location of his target before stepping back outside. He had picked this assignment because it was close to where he already was and because of the particularly high bounty to be found here.

Based on the picture One was provided, Acacia Wickstrom was pretty. She was a high school athlete and went by the name Casey among her peers. Acacia was a pretty name, but a mouthful. One understood the pressure that could come from a name, and how much easier it could be to hide behind a nickname.

It had been a long time since One had worked soul trade, but he still knew the tricks. One wasn't physically superior so he couldn't assume he could take Acacia by brute force. He'd have to come up with something better.

IV

CASEY

Sunrises were Casey's biggest motivator to run in the mornings. With all the colors in the clouds, it looked like a child's video game. In the game she would jump from pink cirrus to deep violet nimbus to sherbet orange stratus clouds, collecting candy XP and power-ups that let her fly. For now, she jogged underneath them, only imagining what it would be like a thousand feet or more in the air along fluffy cumulus clouds, returning to white as the day brightened.

Quiet was the second motivator. When Casey's alarm went off at 5 am, she was the only one awake in her house. Her parents slept on and her brother wouldn't wake up until Casey dragged him out of bed for school — or he slept until midday now that it was summer and a Sunday. Slipping into workout clothes that hugged her body nicely, Casey had the morning to herself. Upbeat music played through her headphones, uninterrupted by texts and notifications. She loved her boyfriend, her best friend, and everyone else in her circle, but the silence of the morning was a nice reprieve.

People were the third motivator. Adults ran in the mornings and Casey loved feeling like one of them. She loved the looks she got from tired, old parents as she whipped past them, curly dark ponytail flying behind her. They were jealous to be that energized again and impressed someone so young had the dedication to be a distance runner.

Casey's mother had expressed her concern countless times about her daughter's morning routine that featured a lot of solitude and contact with strangers. The Wickstrom family lived in a gated, suburban community with a reputation for kind neighbors, but nothing outmatched a mother's worrying. Last year, Casey had been made to carry a whistle while she ran, in case of emergency, but she stopped bringing it after her mother stopped checking. She met the same people along their regular routes every day. If anyone tried to grab her, she knew she was faster than they could hope to be. Casey was her own defense; she didn't need a stupid whistle.

On this particular morning, Casey took steps purely out of habit without much real conviction behind them. Fatigue kept her from focusing on every stride like she wanted to.

Dinner last night with the track team had been a blast, but they had all stayed out a little late. Dylan had found something vegan on the menu, but Rose had tried to tease him about it all night and Casey couldn't move from her spot in between them for fear they might actually start fighting — or worse, flirting.

It wouldn't be the first time Rose had stolen a boy out from under Casey's nose. Technically it had been the boy's fault for cheating so Casey couldn't stay mad at Rose for long. Casey had seen Rose's seduction methods in action before and they weren't to be messed with. Even the young waiter tending to the table of excited track girls and a couple significant others started falling under the blonde's charm. Casey watched him stumble, almost pitying him.

Blinking, Casey realized she'd lost herself in a tired trance, amused to find she'd turned her usual corner on autopilot, increasing her speed to a near sprint for this segment like usual. The sidewalk was devoid of other joggers and dog-walkers, the reason Casey used this block for her sprint.

The sun was starting to heat up the day and she sweated profusely, unzipping her top, a sleeveless blue hooded shirt. With the middle open, her pink sports bra was exposed, but plenty of people ran in minimal clothing, as Casey had tried to persuade her mother when she tried to go out without a real shirt once before. She would zip it back up when she turned the next corner. Or maybe she would leave it open as she passed the college-age guy who she passed on that section every Tuesday, Thursday, and Sunday. Casey had no intention of leaving Dylan, but it was nice to know she still had game.

Zipping around the corner, Casey was disappointed not to see him in the distance. Something must have kept him from his routine. Maybe he was late? Casey slowed her pace, looking around. When she caught sight of the street sign, she stumbled. She wasn't on the correct road for her usual route. Had she taken a wrong turn somewhere? This was her neighborhood and it would take a lot more than a few sleepy mistakes to make her lose her way.

Yet, when she slowed at the next street corner, she didn't recognize the names on the intersecting signs. She had to be really lost if she didn't know the street names. Turning in a full circle, she inspected the houses on both sides of the street. If she was on the correct street, these should've been the same houses she ran past every day, but now she didn't know. It had been a long time since she'd paid any attention to her surroundings on her familiar route.

Up and down blocks, Casey did what she did best. She ran. She looked for any landmarks she could reference to reorient herself, but didn't know what to look for. The street signs were still unmistakably different from what they should've been and Casey didn't figure her fatigue could play with her mind so much as to rearrange words and locations. Panic began its slow creep up Casey's sore legs and settled in her stomach.

In the distance, Casey spotted movement. A few blocks away, a figure stood on the corner of the street, leaning against a stop sign. The chance of finding help renewed Casey's fading fortitude and she jogged toward the person.

As Casey got closer, she reduced her pace to a brisk walk, studying the stranger and the details that came into view. The person hadn't given any indication that he noticed Casey and stood at an angle so she could only make out half his face.

At ten feet away, Casey determined the stranger was taller than her by a few inches, lean with a relaxed, slouched posture. More unusual than his pure white hair were the black jeans, black long-sleeve shirt, white vest, and black scarf he wore, much too warm for the June day still heating up. At five feet away, Casey noted the odd shine in his eyes along with the studs and rings rimming his ear and Casey placed him in the group of kids she saw at school who did their best to be different from everyone else, goth or scene or some other clique Casey didn't associate with. He did a good job of it, Casey thought, stifling the instinct to wrinkle her nose. If Casey wasn't so hopelessly lost, she wouldn't be caught dead talking to someone who looked like that.

"Hi there!" Casey forced a bright smile, hoping she didn't reek of sweat. She had no idea what she was going to say without looking insane or stupid.

The stranger turned to face Casey, stopping her in her tracks. A long, white scar marked the side of his face Casey hadn't seen at first, running several inches long under his left eye.

"Are you stuck here too?" the strange kid spoke, unfazed by whatever expression Casey wore.

"Stuck..." Casey took a hesitant step forward.

"In the neighborhood. Something's wrong. Look."

Was Casey not alone in being lost? Maybe the sinking feeling of dread in her stomach wasn't hers alone. Maybe she wasn't lost in her neighborhood, but her neighborhood lost around her. She approached the stranger, looking at a small device in his hands. It was a compass, Casey realized, not stopping to wonder why he had one. The needle spinning wildly around the face was a more pressing question and Casey exhaled. "What does that mean?"

"I have an idea but it's not good. You're the only other person I've seen all day. Come with me and I'll get us out of here."

Casey found herself following the stranger's steps. Her fear of the situation hadn't subsided, but it felt nice to follow someone offering to carry her to safety. It made her feel a bit like a princess in a movie and she didn't have any better ideas herself. "I'm Casey, by the way. It's nice to meet you."

"Yeah, the track star. I go to West High too. I've seen you around. Call me One. Like the number." One glanced over his shoulder to shoot Casey a glance. He didn't quite smile, but Casey found him charming regardless. The introduction answered a few of Casey's questions, though she still wondered how she could avoid noticing someone at school who looked as distinct as One. With another glance at a misplaced street sign, Casey pushed the doubt out of her mind and followed.

V

ONE

It was freezing on Earth. One pulled the sleeves of his shirt down over his hands. It took more strength than One had been expecting to change the appearance of the signs on the street corners and cloak other pedestrians from mortal eyes, but it had been worth it when Acacia turned a corner and ran straight into One's arms for rescue.

She started talking at once, loud enough to be annoying, but she was scared and clueless, which tended to bring out the worst in people. Seeing her in person was different than the file of information One had on her. She was more animated than One had expected, flicking her hair over her shoulder and talking with her hands. She looked more like an "Acacia" than a "Casey." There was something regal in the way she held herself, like she was above everyone else and impervious to being dragged down to their level. That would soon change.

One stuck to his script. He had brought along a golden compass to drive home the point. It was a celestial compass and wouldn't do much on earth. But it would look confusing, which would convince Acacia something was amiss in her neighborhood. There *was* something amiss, but it went much deeper than incorrect street signs. One had to rely on Acacia to be unobservant and not think too hard. Not many mortals thought very hard about anything.

Movement in One's peripheral vision caught his attention. He was hiding any other pedestrians from Acacia's view to drive home the illusion, but the large-framed man stalking closer was no stranger out for a morning stroll. The same way the people at the bar last night should have no recollection of One, no human should really be paying him any mind as he stood on the street corner. That could only mean that the man wasn't human.

One looked through the information on Acacia that Gogmuth had planted in his mind, then bit back a swear. If he'd paid more attention, he would've noticed Gogmuth had hired three more soul traders in addition to him. The one who successfully brought Acacia in would be paid. The others, if they were lucky enough to survive, would go home empty-handed. The steep reward had clouded One's vision. This job was suicide.

In a flash of panic, One considered running away from Acacia as she spoke. The other three traders were sure to be more experienced in soul trade than One and getting so close to Acacia put One at the top of the kill list. This wasn't worth it.

One cleared his throat, swallowing panic. The ruse was working and the reward was within reach. "Follow me," One murmured. He eyed the broad-shouldered trader and moved in the opposite direction. He looked around again, spotting someone else who looked too casual to be a casual pedestrian. The third trader had to around here somewhere too. One quickened his pace, glancing back at Acacia, following a half-step behind with the most trusting expression on her face.

Stupid, stupid, stupid human. Acacia should never have followed One. This was not going to be a clean hunt. Acacia's naivete would only make One a target for the other traders. He should just give up and relinquish Acacia to one of the others. He could find another job if he backed out of this one, but if he kept this up, his blood would cover the ground sooner or later when he made an inevitable mistake.

One could escape back to his personal realm. It would be warm there and the treasure littering every surface was familiar and comforting. No one and nothing could touch him there... except death. It wouldn't be long before the demon blood ran out and One would die anyway.

With a deep exhale, One released his hold on the mild visual manipulation, letting the street signs go back to normal. As long as One stuck close to Acacia, it was unlikely any of the other soul traders would be able to strike without causing a scene in front of the rest of the neighborhood. One would stick with this hunt. With everything to gain and nothing to lose, it was worth a shot.

VI

CASEY

"Wait..." Casey paused, looking up. "I know this street. Yeah, everything looks normal again. What happened?" While everything looked normal again, it didn't feel right, though it wasn't something Casey could explain in words.

Looking over at her new companion, One didn't look surprised in the slightest. Casey felt on the verge of tears, scared of whatever this was that she couldn't explain, but One maintained the same neutral expression. Either he really wasn't fazed or the real reaction was well hidden under the surface.

A block away, Casey saw her house, exactly where it had always been, but it looked more real than before. She wanted to run home and hug her family as tightly as she could. Just for an instant, she'd lost them but everything was okay now. Casey took a single stride forward before One grabbed her arm.

Casey flinched away from the touch like ice on her bare skin. "Your hands are freezing!"

One retracted his hand but didn't break the intense eye contact. He didn't seem to register Casey's comment. He leaned in, speaking in a low murmur. "You think everything's okay now because it looks normal? You're going to pretend nothing happened just now? You think it's safe?"

The tone of One's voice was a knife pressed against Casey's throat, an invisible threat. Casey hadn't considered *not* trusting One when they'd met on the street corner, but when she looked at him now, she didn't know why she'd followed him. He was creepy. She shouldn't have anything to do with him.

Casey looked around for any familiar nearby pedestrians, fear rising in her chest again as she backed away from One. This was Stranger Danger 101 and Casey had failed.[7]

"Don't freak out, Acacia," One said in the same flat tone of voice. "You're in danger, but I can get you out of here if you follow me."

Staring at One, she felt like his cold hands were closing around her heart, squeezing fear through her body. She hadn't introduced herself with her full name. One had said he knew her from school, but Casey was sure she would remember someone like that and nobody at school called her Acacia. Casey did what she did best. She ran.

One was on her tail, Casey knew, but nobody outran her, especially with this much adrenaline in her system. Home was still two blocks away and Casey didn't want to take any chances. She aimed herself at the nearest pedestrian, a woman with gray hair walking a black terrier. One couldn't do anything to her if she was with an adult.

The woman looked up in surprise as Casey called out to her and stopped.

"Ma'am, please." Casey skidded to a halt. "There's someone after me; you have to help!" When Casey looked over her shoulder, she didn't see One anywhere. Her chest seized up again with fear. The only thing worse than being followed was not knowing where her stalker was. Even if she couldn't see him, he was still out there.

The woman looked concerned. "Are you okay? Who's after you? I have a phone and you can call the police or I can walk you home."

Casey took a grateful step in the direction of her house. She had her phone with her, but she needed someone with her until she was home. She just wanted to be safe from shifting street names and weird strangers. "He said he went to my school..." The fear had turned to nausea in the pit of Casey's stomach the more she thought about this. "But he didn't look like a high schooler. I don't know how old he was. I don't know why I followed him in the first place..."

As tears escaped Casey's eyes, the woman's expression softened as she patted Casey's shoulder. "Maybe I should take you to the police station myself. My car is right over here."

"It's okay, I live just up the street."

But the woman was now standing next to a black car

parked on the curb, holding the passenger door open for Casey. "Quickly, dear. I don't know where your attacker went, but I'm sure he's still close by. You wouldn't want to lead him to your home either in case he's still watching you."

It made sense, what the lady said. The last thing Casey wanted was to put her family in danger too. So focused on escaping One, she hadn't even noticed the woman had a car. She mumbled a quick thank you and climbed into the passenger seat. The woman got behind the wheel and pulled away from the curb.

"Where's your dog?" Casey asked, glancing around the interior of the car.

Without taking her eyes off the road, the woman increased her speed.

Casey's blood ran cold and she started crying again. "Y-you had a little dog with you... I'd like to go home please, ma'am, I'm sorry. It's okay, what I said about the person following me. I need to get home so if you could let me out and I'll walk from here! Please let me out!" Sobs turned to screams and Casey yanked on the handle of the door. It stayed locked. She tried pounding on the window but there was no one outside to notice her. Why would she even get in the car with a stranger in the first place? She had failed Stranger Danger 101 twice in five minutes.[8]

Her eyes catching on something out the front windshield, Casey screamed. They'd traveled two blocks but the white-haired boy was here, standing in the middle of the road. He had both arms outstretched, motioning for the car to stop.

Instead of swerving to avoid a collision, the woman behind the wheel aimed straight at the One and accelerated.

Casey screamed again and lunged across the car, yanking the wheel away from her kidnapper and driving the car into the sidewalk. She was thrown back in her seat as the front of the car connected with a street lamp pole and the airbags went off.

Casey struggled against the seatbelt and the deflating airbag. Her phone had tumbled out of her pocket and lay on the floor, out of reach no matter how far she stretched. She wasn't sure if she'd blacked out or not, but the woman beside her was groaning and Casey wasn't about to wait for her to come to her senses.

A click beside her drew Casey's attention and she saw her door open as One leaned in, offering a hand, forehead creased with worry. "Are you okay?"

Casey nodded and stumbled out, clutching One's hands, not caring that they were cold. "You were right; I'm sorry for running away! What's happening?"

"I'll explain later." One hurried to back away from the car. The driver side door opened and the woman stepped out. There was blood down the side of her enraged face.

One shifted into a defensive stance. "Back off. You lost.

Take your loss honorably and I won't worry about revenge."

The woman raised her arm, clutching a gun.

Casey didn't even have time to scream before One grabbed her. Instead of keeping her safe or shielding her somehow, the mysterious savior pulled Casey in front of him, pushing her toward the gunwoman. Casey could see the whites of the woman's eyes by the time One let her go. She pulled away, flinging herself at the ground as the gun went off.

Blood, warm and dark splattered on Casey, marking her arm and face. Afraid of what she might see when she turned, she blinked up at the scene in front of her. The woman's shot had gone off somewhere in the sky; One was clutching her gun hand and pointing it straight up. The woman's other hand was wrapped around One's throat weakly, her eyes bugged out. The rest of her was obscured behind One's body, positioned to block Casey's view.

One glanced at Casey before letting go of the woman. Her lifeless body hit the asphalt with a dull smack like a sack of old fruit, blood gushing from a wound in the center of her chest.

As One turned back toward her, Casey saw in his other hand, something that looked like a large nail, coated with blood, the vile liquid covering most of One's hand as well. The air between them was quiet enough for Casey to hear the soft splatters of blood dripping off One's hand and hitting the asphalt.

VII

ONE

Murder.

One thought he was going to be sick. The woman's blood on his hand was pleasantly warm but the sight of her body on the ground, twisted and ripped open was anything but pleasant.

The crucifix nail had claimed a victim, something it hadn't done for years. If the ragged point of the tool had feelings, One figured it might be excited to be involved in death again. Even after being pried off the cross, and being lost to time and treasure hunters, it had witnessed some significant lives lost over the centuries. One wasn't sure the blade *didn't* feel, a hunger for blood that could only be denied for so long.

The wound in the woman's chest steamed as the blood flow weakened. Immortal weapons didn't work the same as any normal device did. They were extremely rare and valuable, significant because they had touched Christ and gained powers from the encounter. Any wound from an immortal weapon was fatal for demons, no matter where they were hit. Objects that had come into physical contact with Christ were deadly to celestial creatures. This was the primary reason no demon would form a communication link with someone holding an immortal weapon. The spear that had pierced Christ's side had become legendary on its own, being the cause of death of thousands of demons over the years.

For humans, the damage wasn't quite as severe, but still a step more extreme than a normal injury. As with the man at the bar One had casually cut the night before, wounds from the holy nails never healed properly, a constant and painful reminder of the injury. One had woken up with a shred of remorse for hurting an innocent man, but there was nothing to be done about it now.

An unholy mix between demons and humans were paramortals, people like One who enhanced their normal abilities with demon blood. The damage done to a paramortal by a holy weapon fell in the middle of the spectrum, varying on how much demon blood was coursing through their veins. One had stabbed the trader through the heart, enough to kill a human, but it was clear by the wound that she'd had a lot of demon blood in her system. Black and tar-like, demon blood mixed with human blood caked the edges of the wound, bubbling lazily to the surface, still steaming and putting off an odor of rot.

As unpleasant as it was to get closer, One stooped next to the woman and went through the pockets of her pants. If she carried any vials of demon blood with her, One could easily steal those and ditch this entire soul trade endeavor. Acacia would fall victim to one of the other two traders and One could back out of this sick game. Time would bring him another hunt for relics or angel feathers if he had enough demon blood to survive the wait.

But the trader was likely no stranger to these high-risk missions and was smart enough not to carry something as valuable as demon blood with her in the open. One still kept the remaining half-vial zipped into the pocket of his now blood-soaked white vest, afraid to let it out of his sight.

Trying not to vomit at the stench of rotting demon blood, One saw the look of horror on Acacia's tear-streaked face as she stared at the body. One stood up and nudged the dead woman's arm with the toe of a sneakered foot. "See the gross black stuff in her chest? She's not human."

Acacia turned an impossible shade paler. "What is she?"

"Part demon." There wasn't any use in lying about that. If anything, cluing Acacia in on the details of her attempted kidnapping would add credibility to his story. If she was as naive as One thought, this alone might convince her to follow him without questioning One's motives. Taking the competition into consideration, One had enough on his hands to worry about without Acacia trying to escape.

"S-she was trying to hurt me?"

One nodded, backing away from the body. "Yes. Now do

you believe me?"

Acacia's eyes narrowed and she snapped out of her horrified shock. "Hold on, you're not any better! You used me as a shield!"

Sighing, One walked slowly away, waiting for Acacia to follow. "She wouldn't have risked shooting you. She was trying to deliver you to a demon who put out a bounty on you and it would've killed her chance if you were dead." The girl didn't need to know One was operating on the exact same agenda. "You're welcome for saving your life."

"I saved you too!" Acacia stood still rooted to her spot on the sidewalk. "She was going to hit you with her car!"

One turned and gave Acacia the biggest eye-roll he could manage. "You think my plan was to stand in the middle of the road and get hit by a car? I had something in mind, you just... did it your own way."

"I saved myself then." The triumphant look on Acacia's face made One want to vomit worse than the smell of demon blood. Coming from the mouth of such a self-important human who had walked straight into disaster, she sounded like a child bragging about blowing out the birthday candles on her cake by herself — outside on a windy day.

"Alright, that's fine. You saved yourself once and you'll do it again." One turned away but didn't leave.

Acacia took a hesitant step away from the body in the street. "What's going to happen to her?"

"Which part? Her soul is already facing the worst torments of hell. Her body will be swept up at some point. Whoever finds her won't register her as a human being and they won't be any more suspicious than if they found a pile of trash in the road. Don't ask me how the science of that works, but trust me that it does. She won't be bothering anyone anymore."

"What about me? Are you going to take me home?"

"No," One replied honestly, turning to face her. "I'm going to take you far away. There are at least two more soul traders like that lady after you and we need to get away from them."

"Two more like her?" Acacia ran to fall into step beside One.

Satisfaction with the plan lifted some of the weight One carried. Acacia wasn't going to be a liability in this journey. "There are two more traders that I know of. I saw one of them earlier, but I lost track after I started following you in the car. I haven't seen the other one at all so it's more likely that they'll stay hidden until the timing is right to strike. And it's entirely possible more have picked up on the hunt." That fact put the stress right back down One's shoulders.

"So... you're here to kill them until it's safe for me to go home?"

Despite the situation, when One looked over at Acacia, he saw a hopeful smile beginning to pull at her face. She was in mortal danger and knew it, but the emotion she held onto was positive. There was no place for gullibility in this world, but the part of One that wished hope was real didn't want to lie to her. "It's up to you if you trust me. I can die about as easily as you can, but I probably have a better shot at killing them than you do. It's your choice though; I can't make you stay with me."

Acacia nodded slowly, wrapping her mind around the concept. Hopefully, she would be too overwhelmed to consider her savior as a threat.

VIII

CASEY

Watching One remain so calm through this whole experience made Casey wonder if it was something he dealt with regularly. It sure appeared like he did; the white-haired stranger had killed the demon lady without breaking a sweat.

Maybe fairy tale heroes did exist, but they didn't look like knights or princes. Maybe they looked like One, a little odd, but ready to jump into a situation Casey never would've escaped on her own, slaying the monster and sweeping Casey off her feet. Well, One didn't seem the type for sweeping people off their feet, but there were less attractive heroes to be rescued by. Casey figured she could do worse. One wore sweaters and scarves in June and didn't like to meet her eye. On the other hand, Dylan had an affinity for whining and religiously watched his calories. No one was perfect, but One wasn't too far off.

"So how do you know so much about me? No one calls me Acacia." Casey jogged to keep up, staying on the side of One that wasn't marked with the scar under his eye. It was easier to see the valiant hero type without the ugly mark making him look like a villain instead.

"You think I happened to stumble upon you while you were being attacked by half-demons?" One scoffed. "And is that the most pressing question you have?"

"What do you mean?" Casey wanted to get to know her mysterious rescuer before she put her whole trust in him, so yes, it was a pressing question.

"Most people start with 'Demons are real?' before they ask where I got my intel."

Casey fell quiet. One was right, of course, but there were far too many questions she wanted answered to even consider organizing them by priority. If Casey thought too hard about her current situation — following a stranger she just met to an unknown safe location while trying not to be kidnapped by the part-demons chasing her — she thought she might cry again. "That's an obvious answer. Do I have a limited number of questions I get to ask or something?"

"Until I get bored of listening to you talk."

A faint smile crept onto Casey's lips. Despite the cold delivery, Casey found One's wry humor kind of cute. "Okay then, why are you dressed like it's winter?"

"It's better than how you're dressed."

Casey looked down. Her blue sleeveless hoodie shirt was still unzipped from her run, showing off her pink sports bra.

With an embarrassed squeak, she hurried to fix the zipper. She was pretty sure fairy tale princesses never accidentally flashed their knight in shining armor, but she hoped One could overlook that detail if she brushed it off. "Aren't you warm in that though? And your hands are cold."

Shifting his hands into the pockets of his jeans, One shrugged. "Earth is cold. I tend to spend my time somewhere a little warmer."

As frustrating as the vague answers were, Casey had to admit the mysterious vibe emanating from One was exciting, like he really was some fantastical hero bent on saving her life. "So the things chasing me are half-demons trying to capture me for their master? What happens if they win? Will the demon kill me?"

"Couldn't tell you. It depends on the demon."

"Who are you in all of this? If you're fighting against the demons, are you an angel?"

One looked away."Do I look like an angel to you?" Was he too shy or too modest to answer that?

"Part-angel then?" That option made the most sense to Casey as the only true adversary for a part-demon. The fairy tale kept getting better and better. Casey had never spent much time considering the possibility of a guardian angel alongside her.[9] As a kid, of course, she probably believed it the way she believed the sun would always rise and Santa Claus brought her toys on Christmas morning. She remembered

Sunday School lessons about angels and wondered when she had stopped believing in the celestial being that walked next to her no matter where she went. Maybe her guardian angel had disappeared with the rest of her childhood imaginary friends. Maybe the fantasy faded when her family stopped going to church every Sunday morning. She still considered herself a Christian, but couldn't remember the last time she'd been to church that wasn't Christmas or Easter. Maybe she'd left the belief of guardian angels behind on the steps into the sanctuary she never visited anymore.

Once she got out of this situation, she'd go back and thank God for sending a guardian angel to save her when she needed it most. The fact that God had never abandoned her even though she wasn't the most devout follower made Casey feel bad.[10]

Swallowing back tears that threatened her honey-brown eyes, Casey wrung her hands, wondering if it would be out of line to go to church right now. It was a Sunday morning after all and what safer place could she find to hide from demons than in a church? "One? Are we in a hurry or can we make a stop?"

One raised an eyebrow at Casey. "The other traders will have an easier time catching up if we're not moving. What kind of stop do you want to make?"

"Never mind," Casey said. "Maybe this is another stupid question, but where are you taking me?"

"The light rail station. The safe house is downtown and that's the fastest way to get there short of stealing a car."

Lost in thought and fairy tales, Casey had barely realized they were still walking. The two had left the neighborhood behind and continued at a brisk pace down the street, cars whizzing past in both directions.

Lingering paranoia made Casey check her surroundings. Plenty of people were out in plain view and none of them looked suspicious. Then again, neither had the lady who had tricked Casey into her car to be kidnapped. "Are the other half-demons still following us?" she whispered.

"Somewhere. I doubt they would've been scared off for long, but they'll avoid a fight if they can. Our best bet is to keep moving toward where we need to be."

IX

ONE

Careful to avoid eye contact, One only glanced at Acacia when she was faced away. Her head moved on a swivel as if she would be able to spot a paramortal soul trader trying not to be seen. One didn't pay much mind to the outside world. He needed to reconstruct his plan for safely delivering Acacia and figured he could trust Acacia to scream if someone ran toward them. Ready for anything, One kept his hand locked around the holy nail in his jeans pocket, still sticky with blood.

The list of things One needed to take care of kept growing, but he would have to wait until Acacia wasn't exposed in the street.

One's white vest was still dipped in red from the battle with the female trader, reeking of demon. He wasn't worried about being stopped by a suspicious human. Anyone who noticed the bloodstained attire wouldn't register it as anything important, the same way One was meaningless to the bartender last night who should've checked for an ID or charged him for the shots.

The same way the dead trader's body would be found and disposed of without causing any head turning.

The real danger came from the celestial world. The smell of demon was distinct and powerful to those who had the ability to sense it. The other paramortals didn't need to have eyes on Acacia to follow her when they could smell One from a mile away. This game wasn't getting any easier and One swore for the hundredth time today that he would never work soul trade again. It was too messy with too many chances for things to go terribly wrong.

Wordlessly, One increased his pace as the train station came into view, the same he'd left the previous night after fleeing from his last assignment. Glancing over while Acacia was distracted again, One read her body language. She was leaving more space between One and herself and the slew of random questions had faded. She no longer looked up at him every couple seconds, hoping to make a friendly connection. When One held the door of the small train station open for Acacia, he was expecting her next words.

"I don't know if I should be here," she said, a tremble in her voice. "I want to go home."

One sighed, readying the web of half-truths he was willing to tell Acacia. "I told you, I can't force you to come with me. I think we both know you can outrun me. If you turn back, I can't stop you and I'm not even going to try, but you're on your own. You don't have to believe a word I'm saying; that's a risk you'll take. I have no influence over what happens to you if you leave me and I won't be able to do much to save you if something happens."

Dark eyes narrowing, Acacia crossed her arms. "Is that a threat? I don't need to listen to this story you're feeding me! Maybe that lady was trying to kidnap me, but how do I know if I'm really safe with you either? Give me proof that you're actually trying to save me!"

"I can't," One said, gesturing with his blood-covered hands. "I have no proof to give you. It's up to you to decide where you want to be because I'm not forcing you to do anything. I need to go wash up anyway and I'll leave you right here by yourself with plenty of chances to escape if that makes you feel better."

A split had started forming in One's mind as he walked to the train station. He wanted the reward for Acacia's capture, wanted to stay alive, but another part of him wanted to give up before he was killed. Even with the first trader dead, he was horribly outmatched and he didn't know all the details of the assignment. Part of him wanted another of the traders to snatch Acacia away while he wasn't looking so it wasn't his fault for giving up, for dying. He needed to change clothes and brush up on the details of the file. He would let fate decide whether Acacia would still be there when he was finished.

"What if one of the traders comes for me while you're gone?"

"Hide or something. I mean it when I say your life is in your own hands." One nodded at a sign for restrooms and took a step away. "I'll be back in a few minutes."

Acacia stood, stuck in place, staring with wide eyes as One disappeared behind a wall and left her alone, exposed, and vulnerable.

Transported instantly to the illusionary realm One called home, he sank to his knees, finally able to let his guard down for a moment, releasing the tension knotting in his shoulders.

The longer One spent on Earth, the more welcoming home felt. After this job was complete, he would take some time to relax before looking for work again. The bounty would support him for a while if he got it. There was no use taking time now to think of what he would do if he failed.

However, home wasn't as welcoming as One was used to. The realm was a product of One's demonic abilities and it depended on his paramortality to exist. It had been hours since the last dose of demon blood One had taken and the withdrawal effects had been hitting him for days. The state of the house was changing as well. Aside from the apparent earthquake that had knocked gold trinkets off shelves and tables, rooms had started shifting their placement, getting One lost on his way to the bathroom.

Staring into the mirror misplaced on the floor instead of the wall, One exhaled. The next time he stepped into the realm, the world might not look anything how One intended it to be.

He might not be able to find his way out. He might not be able to find his way *in*. It depended on how far One could stretch this demon blood and how little was too little. It made him consider never leaving, never stepping back outside, content to run out of demon blood and die in here.

Scrubbing blood off his hands and the crucifix nail, One accessed the case file on Acacia's capture, then swore. To place a bounty on a human soul, demons were required to mark the priority level of the catch. Low-priority souls usually didn't have a faith background and had no means of fighting back against demonic influence. High-priority souls were trickier in every way. They were usually people on the fence of religion. Even they didn't know if they really believed and it made them valuable. Because of the increased urgency to bring in high-priority souls, it was common for a demon to hire several soul traders at a time to pursue the target as in Acacia's instance. Only the trader who succeeded in delivering the soul would be paid and the others would be lucky to survive the high-stakes competition.

The danger involved in high-priority bounties kept some of the best trader away, some preferring to take exclusive jobs and avoid the risks of competition. One fell under that category, hoping for an easy job to complete alone. Had it not been so long since the last time he'd worked soul trade jobs, One might have remembered demons had the tendency to lie.

The ridiculously high bounty should've been an indicator

to One that this was no ordinary low-risk soul trade job and there would probably be other traders to contend with, but he hadn't thought that far. The promise of so much demon blood in payment had gone straight to his head.

At this point, knowing there were other traders on Acacia's tail wasn't new information to One, but it made him stop and question, "was it really worth it?" Leaving Acacia alone in the light rail station was about the riskiest move One could make, but he couldn't be bothered to care. Everything was different when his life came down to this one job.

For the time being, the blood covering his clothes was a pretty big problem on One's platter, but the table was set with infinite dishes of challenges and questions and hard decisions. One stood up again. He needed to decide where to start and move quickly.

Tempting as it was to lie down and take a nap, One padded up the stairs to his bedroom, exchanging his splattered jeans for a clean pair and the puff vest for fleece, hoping it was similar enough that Acacia wouldn't notice.

For the more pressing issue, One transferred the tiny vial of demon blood from the soiled jacket, pausing with it in his hand. At most, three doses were left. One would need to ration them carefully, but he would need to be as strong as possible if he was going to have to fight the entire way to the final destination, the trade house where Acacia would be handed off to Gogmuth.

There was no time to make it pleasant. One didn't keep alcohol on hand at home after too many nights he couldn't remember, his paramortal soul craving release while his human body was driven to the brink of death with empty bottles littering the floor.

Sucking in a few deep breaths in preparation, One tipped his head back and raised the vial to tap a single drop onto his tongue. It burned and One bit back a yell. It didn't help that he hadn't eaten anything recently to feed his human side, meaning the only contents of his stomach were demon blood. The vile liquid spread like fire through One's veins, filling him with power he would never give up.

Doing his best to ignore the stabbing pain, One left the bedroom, taking a moment to look at the other doors, shut and silent. The realm had stabilized somewhat with One's paramortality renewed and he could make it back to the front door without tripping through a random sequence of rooms to get there. With luck, he could find the chance to eat and sleep on the train if it was safe. Rest always helped settle the poison One was addicted to.

One thought through an empty, unheard plea that Acacia would still be there, safe and unstolen, then stepped back out of his realm into the real world.

X

CASEY

"I thought I told you to hide."

Casey whirled around at the sound of One's voice, her shoulders relaxing. "I, uh... got worried about you." Casey glanced at the restrooms, wondering how One had appeared behind her. "I thought you were going to wash up."

"I did." One showed both sides of his hands, cleaned of blood. "I have my ways. You wouldn't understand."

One's changed vest didn't escape Casey's attention either as she examined him. None of it added up, but One was full of mysteries Casey couldn't fathom the answers to. She wondered if guardian angels were able to use public bathrooms or if One had vanished to some heavenly washroom to clean up.

A hint of amusement laced One's casual shrug as he headed toward the ticket window. "Considering you're still here, I take it you're coming with me?"

Casey followed without replying. Every feeling in her heart was all mixed up. She wanted to trust One but wasn't sure if it was wise. She had just met him and he had yet to give her a straight answer or a solid reason to believe his story. For all Casey knew, One was mentally deranged and had made up the angels and demons story, dragging her into the fantasy world in his head. One had even killed a lady without looking remorseful. But Casey couldn't deny that the now-dead woman had tried to take her much more sneakily, tempting her into the car. One had never tried to trick Casey as far as she knew.

She would be stupid to ignore the signs she was in danger. Casey wasn't sure what she had ever done to warrant being targeted by a demon, but she wasn't exactly an expert in that field. However, she was in the presence of someone who was an expert and Casey figured that would be the safest place for her. She knew she couldn't hope to defeat or outrun this danger on her own. Yet, there was a certain edgy vibe to her new companion that Casey didn't trust. She couldn't imagine a half angel wearing so much black or baring such an ugly scar on their face or littering their ear with piercings, but then again, what did Casey know about angels?

Making up her mind, Casey stood next to One at the ticket window, receiving a card of thick paper, printed with the date, time, and destination of the train. She could still outrun One if she needed to, but for now, she was content to trust him.

The light rail train was several cars long and One picked the last seats in the last segment when they boarded. Minutes later, the train left, heading toward the stop downtown in the nearest major city, about fifteen minutes away.

One shifted in his seat as the train pulled away. It was almost imperceptible, but Casey thought she saw his shoulders relax a bit. She hadn't taken her eyes off her guardian angel since One had returned from cleaning up. He didn't put off much body language, but Casey was figuring out how to interpret what she could see. The way One's blue eyes flicked over every surface, window, and person in his surroundings all while maintaining an appearance of being focused straight ahead was uncanny but Casey thought it was interesting and a bit artistic.

Since they'd reunited, there was something different about the way One held himself. It was a confidence or sense of control that hadn't been there when he'd trudged into the train station. It was an aura of strength, but it wasn't an effortless strength. This newfound control was the only thing holding him together, and it was straining him.

As the train left the station behind, One let go of the tense silence. "How are you holding up?"

It was a surprisingly caring question, considering how emotionless One's demeanor appeared. "I'm okay," Casey mumbled. "If I try really hard, I can pretend I'm going downtown for the day with a friend, not being hunted."

"If you're tired, you can sleep on the way."

Casey flinched away. It was barely noon. "I'm not going to

sleep! I don't trust you!"

One held his hands up in surrender, shifting away. "Sorry. I thought you might be stressed. I'm going to close my eyes so wake me up if you need anything."

Casey nodded and turned her head out the window, keeping her peripheral vision trained on One.

He didn't seem to have any trouble sleeping in the bench seat, his breathing slow and his face relaxed. He looked soft, and maybe even a little vulnerable. Casey didn't hide her gaze in the window anymore as she watched him, wondering about the stranger's past. He had been there when she ran at dawn, earlier than the rest of the world cared to wake up. Maybe angels didn't need to sleep, but One looked so human, so tired.

It almost made Casey feel bad, but not quite. She shifted silently, looking One up and down once more before lightly touching his white fleece vest and inching the zippered pockets open.

So far, Casey had more questions than answers about her companion's identity. She'd feel a lot more secure if she had some indication of who One really was and where he had come from before appearing so suddenly in her life.

The pocket was empty. No wallet, no ID, no keys or anything normal people carried in their coats. Casey leaned over One to carefully check the next pocket. Though it wasn't what she'd been aiming for, Casey found a clue. A thin, glass vial came out of the pocket and Casey glanced at One's face to verify he was still sleeping before she examined it. The glass tube was incredibly thin and filled about a half inch full, a quarter of the total length. A black stopper capped the tube, containing a few drops of a black liquid.

Casey tried to justify it as an angel thing, but the tiny vial seemed to give off the same ominous aura One did. It was something she shouldn't be holding, something a guardian angel shouldn't be hiding in their pocket.

If need be, Casey could probably use this against One. She slid the vial into her own pocket and kept moving. One's jeans were tight and it made Casey nervous to be searching her fingers into the pockets, but he was dead to the world, fast asleep. Again, her search for an ID of some sort came up empty, One's pants contained only the train ticket and the nail he'd used earlier.

The weight of the weapon in Casey's hands felt as dangerous as the vial. She should not be holding this unless she wanted to share in the bloodlust of One's danger-filled, demon-fighting world. Still, it was too intriguing to put back down. It didn't look sharp or dangerous. Earlier, dripping with blood in One's hand, it had looked like a dagger, but Casey couldn't see it as anything more than a large nail that belonged in a museum. Though Casey had seen it stab someone through the heart, it looked like it would disintegrate to the touch.

Casey slipped it into her pocket as well in case of emergency.

The door at the front of the train car opened and a large man in a gray suit stepped through. He walked through the nearly empty car and stopped beside Casey's seat. "Tickets?"

Scrambling to hand over her ticket, Casey gingerly took One's ticket and handed it over too. As she leaned over her companion into the aisle, the large man grabbed her arm. Before she had a chance to scream, his other hand covered her mouth and she was yanked out of the seat.

Casey did her best to kick out and grab One's attention, but she was already being dragged down the center aisle of the train car. In seconds, Casey had been pulled through the back door of the train into an electrical closet full of switches and readouts, monitoring how the train ran along its route. A window in the back emergency door showed the tracks beneath the train as they raced toward the city.

Frantically, Casey scrabbled against the man's grip, but she wouldn't be escaping on her own. A spark of inspiration kicked in and Casey remembered the oversized nail she'd looted from One's pocket. She ripped it back out and drove the point into her attacker's arm around her.

The point of the nail hit home, but the man's grip didn't falter. The weapon had disposed of the first lady so efficiently and Casey couldn't understand why it hadn't worked this time. Despair made the nail drop from Casey's fingers onto the floor. Then she looked at the man's arms as they tightened around her. He wasn't wearing gray, he *was* gray. What Casey had assumed to be a gray jacket was dull silver steel and the darker shade of his skin was copper. For a split second, Casey made contact with the human eyes staring out of a mechanical face before she was thrown against the wall in silent anger, hard enough for her vision to go black until she hit the floor.

Blinking away tears of pain and terror, Casey looked up at the metal man. If he was made of flesh and bone, he would still be considered large, towering over Casey and weighing at least 250 pounds. His copper plated hands were the size of Casey's head, clicking softly as they curled into fists at his sides.

The nail. Where was One's nail?

Casey knew she would need a stronger weapon to pierce the trader's metal skin, but it was still her best shot until the man plucked it off the floor before she could grab it.

Without breaking his stare he tucked it into a pocket in the outer shell of his legs, a complex, metal mess. Real fear touched Casey again. One had said the soul traders wouldn't try to hurt her; they were delivering her to a demon. The throbbing pain in Casey's entire body from being thrown said otherwise. With the man's eyes on her, Casey closed her own, deciding the most effective thing she could do was pray. God had sent her a guardian angel and He could deliver her from this too.[11]

XI

ONE

The slamming of the door opened One's eyes again and he cursed immediately at the empty seat next to him. He didn't even need to pat his pockets to know the crucifix nail and the vial of blood were gone. The question was if Acacia had taken them or another trader — and if Acacia had run away of her own accord or if she had been taken.

One looked up and down the aisle, feeling absolutely imbecilic as he got to his feet. He wasn't a heavy sleeper normally, but he had also been without quality rest for days now, on the hunt for a reliable supply of demon blood. And without the effects of regular tastes of the celestial liquid, the consequences of the sleepless nights were catching up. Had he been a heavy sleeper back when he was human? One couldn't remember; it had been too long since mortality had enforced a strict sleep requirement on him.

Even anticipating withdrawal symptoms, sleeping on the job should never have happened. He had only meant to close his eyes to make Acacia feel less threatened and shake some of the echoes of pain from drinking straight demon blood. With the number of mistakes he'd been making, soul trade was going to get One killed before it brought him a profit.[12] Never again.

The door at the back of the train car was locked and the window was blocked by something large. The sinking feeling seeped through One. Another trader was on the train and had taken Acacia. They were already on the way to the drop off point where Gogmuth wanted the girl delivered so there was no use in escaping the train. All the trader needed to do was keep Acacia nearby and deal with One when he presented himself as a problem. Now that he had his hands on Acacia, this paramortal would be hard to take down. He wouldn't let her out of his sight until she was trapped inside a pentagram, awaiting Gogmuth.

One considered making the train crash since that plan had already worked once that day. There probably was a way to accomplish it, but One couldn't guarantee Acacia's safety and everything was pointless if she was killed.

Without the crucifix nail, One didn't have any leverage. Under normal circumstances, One would've popped into his home realm and found another weapon. His home was full of them, none so powerful as the holy nail, but still effective. But without the demon blood, a jump into the separate realm came with the risk of getting stuck or lost in the world of One's creation.

The most effective weapon One had was Acacia herself. As long as she was unharmed, she would run away from the other trader. Assuming she still believed One's ruse, she would run straight back to him as soon as she had the opportunity.

The improvised plan felt foolish even to One as he thought it up. He stepped up to the closed back door of the train car and knocked.

The large man shifted away from the window and One recognized him as the other trader he'd glimpsed earlier on Acacia's street. One would need Acacia to escape on her own; he wouldn't be able to win a fight against a trader so large and imposing. The door slid open and One took a step forward, a grin stretching across his face as he adopted the most annoying attitude he could muster. "Morning."

The large man's scowl didn't flicker.

"Hey, come on, nothing?" One tapped the man's arms, folded across his chest. Metal? Inhuman strength of some sort wasn't an uncommon trait to find in paramortals, but this was going to be a challenge One hadn't expected. He modified the plan to fit the circumstance and pressed on. "No reaction? No taunt? You're not even going to try and kill me?"

Eyes narrowing, the man stepped back and glanced over his shoulder, giving One all the confirmation he needed to be positive Acacia was somewhere in that room.

"You don't want to fight? You seem like the kind of guy who would be into that," One teased, matching him with a step forward. "What's the point of soul trade if you're not going to have some fun with it every once in a while? I know you. You're practically famous. No one wins against you which is why I'm going to be the one to kick your ass."

Nothing.

"Really? I didn't take you for a coward. I mean, I doubt you've heard of me before, but I have some special abilities of my own you might like to see. We're even in the perfect setting for it, you know? It's like in movies where they, like, fight to the death on top of a train? I'll give you a head start and everything. Meet you on top?"

Finally, the burly man took a step toward One. "Go home, little treasure hunter. This is not your ring to fight in."

"You do know who I am?" The surprise in One's tone wasn't faked. He had thought he was good enough to stay off the radars of soul traders. Over the man's shoulder, One spotted a flash of movement and hoped Acacia would be smart enough to take the opportunity for escape. There was certain to be an emergency exit in the back of the train and the safest place for her would be on top of the train, out of the way.

"No." Another step into the main car forced One to stumble backward. "But I know a relic collector when I see one. What made you want a job like this, I don't know. But you will not make that mistake again."

"You have something of mine, I think." One noted the end of the nail sticking out of where the man's pants pocket would have been if his legs and everything else weren't made of gray steel. "I can totally fight you without it, but if you wanted it to be a fair fight, you could give that back to me and it would be even cooler."

A faint click sound made the man whirl around. One could barely see around his sizable form, but the open back door flooded the room with daylight.

Soul traders in a race for a bounty tended to see only each other as threats. They never considered their target's ability to fight back. That had been the downfall of the trader earlier in the morning and it would be this man's downfall as well. One had treated victims the same way a long time ago before learning that he had been missing out on a great tool in his arsenal.

The large man struggled to turn around in the small doorway, a key detail that only made the plan better. As he lumbered into the small back room, he kept his arms out, preventing One from darting between him and Acacia. That was fine. One was right where he wanted to be: with the trader between him and the train tracks.

One followed the man as he leaned out the back door. There was no platform, no railing, nothing to catch him. Keeping just behind the man, One heard Acacia scream from above as the metal man twisted around and reached up. One could only hope he didn't have a hold on her as One kicked him in the knee and he stumbled.

The man had completely disregarded One in his search for Acacia again, underestimating the strength of a 'little treasure hunter' and his eyes widened with shock. His large, copper hand dropped to his pocket and he grabbed the holy nail; whatever weapon he usually wielded was a toy compared to the rare immortal artifact.

One lunged for the nail, kicking out again. His mouth opening without sound, the man's fragile stance in the empty doorway gave out. He fell from the back of the train and hit the rails, the sound drowned out by the roar and rumble of the train already flying away from its lost passenger, stopping for no such tragedy as the death of a half-man. One inhaled. That plan could've gone wrong in so many ways. Slowly, he replaced the nail in his pocket, inched out of the doorway, and looked up.

Attached to the back end of the train was a thin, metal ladder that trailed up over the top of the metal box. Arms locked around the top rung, Acacia looked down at One, tears running down her face. One silently thanked God she was alright.

XII

CASEY

"You okay?" One asked, bracing his arms against the open doorway as the train shook and shuddered over the rails. Casey's eyes flicked between One and the body on the rails behind them, getting smaller with distance.

Casey shook her head. "Is he going to get up and keep chasing us? It wasn't that far of a fall and he was really strong so he's probably fine and he's never going to give up until he finds me and he's going to hurt me again or kill you and I can't protect myself from someone like that! He was so big and his skin was like metal and--" Casey's words melted into messy sobs as she clung tighter to the ladder, the only thing in her life she knew was real right now. "I want to go home! I want this to be over so I can see my family and my friends and I don't have to be so scared! I don't know what to do! I've never dreamed of this happening and I'm so afraid to die like this!"

One adjusted his stance to lean further out the train. His voice was calm and quiet as always, like nothing out of the ordinary had happened. "Acacia. That man can't hurt you. He's dead."

"He can't be! We're not safe! We're never going to be safe! He's going to get up and follow us!"

"We're on a light rail train, the tracks have thousands of volts of electricity running through them, and he's made of metal. He's dead. You can come down from there now."

It was a funny feeling to be relieved at the news of someone's death. Casey didn't think she'd ever felt happy at the prospect of death, but she'd also never been kidnapped and beaten and taken to a demon before. She clung tighter to the ladder, the prospect of falling holding new danger.

One held a hand out, his white hair blowing wildly around his face. "I'm not going to let you fall, Acacia."

Step by step, Casey climbed down, One's cold hand on her back to guide her safely onto the train. Casey jumped the last step, not wanting to touch where the burly metal man had stood to take his last breath. Feet connecting with metal flooring, Casey fell into One, throwing her arms around his shoulders and holding on just as tightly as she had to the ladder outside.

One shifted uncomfortably, closing the outside door and cutting off the roaring wind, leaving the small electrical closet silent aside from Casey's ragged breathing.

"Please hold me," Casey whispered. "I've never been so scared in my life."

Hesitantly, One shifted to wrap Casey in a loose hug.

He was still cold. Casey could feel his hands on her back, through her shirt, but it wasn't an unwelcome feeling. One's kind of cold hug was less like a winter day and more like lying down on silk sheets, soft and cool to the touch. It was comfortable and Casey rested her head on One's shoulder. "You don't have to use my full name, you know. All my friends call me Casey." Immediately, Casey could hear One's voice in her mind asking if that was really the most important thing she had to say, considering the circumstances. Casey thought it might be.

"I don't usually use nicknames," One answered bluntly, holding still.

For some reason, it made Casey smile. "Do you call all your friends by their full names or I am I not a friend to you yet?"

"Truthfully, I don't have many friends and I prefer to stick with given names. Once I know someone's name, I don't like to change what I call them."

Casey laughed into One's shoulder, clutching him tighter. She couldn't deny her mind the daydream of One as a guardian angel secret agent, receiving her file as a person of interest, someone the demon-people were after, then refusing to know her by anything other than the name in the file even though she thought by this point she had to be more than that. One was very formal like that, Casey was finding, playing by the rules and never getting flustered when things didn't go to plan.

She didn't mind One using her full name either; it sounded nice in One's quiet, mid-range voice. Casey had always thought her name was pretty, but enough people failed to pronounce it correctly that her nickname had become standard. But if One wanted to call her Acacia, she wouldn't protest it.

Her breathing finally under control, Casey exhaled and pulled out of the hug. One let go as well, a little too eagerly. Casey trailed back to the far door, her legs still feeling weak from the adventure and her shoulder a little sore from being thrown against the wall. It didn't matter anymore. One wasn't going to let anyone touch her again.

Sitting back down in their seats, Casey stayed close to her companion, letting their shoulders touch. One glanced around the train car while maintaining an appearance of staring straight ahead.

Casey looked around as well, noting the distinct lack of anyone else trying to kidnap her. They were out of danger now and One could stand to look a little less tense, be a little less formal. "You use a nickname," Casey commented quietly. "One can't be your real name; nobody names their kid after a number."

"I don't have any other names. It's who I am."

Casey sighed, letting her eyes wander to the window. She estimated they were about five minutes from the stop downtown. One hadn't looked at her again, still scanning the train's interior. "You can relax, One. You said it yourself, that guy is dead and we're safe."

One only shook his head. "We are not safe until this is over. There is a third trader. If I haven't seen them so far it's because they're very good at hiding, not because they're gone. I'm not going to drop my guard until I know who they are and they're dead or we reach the destination first."

None of the other patrons aboard the train looked suspicious to Casey, but she had been wrong before. "I have a question. That guy. He just grabbed me and dragged me into the back and no one else seemed to care. Nobody came to help except you and no one looks like they noticed anything, but wouldn't that have been pretty obvious?"

Finally, One looked down at Casey. "It's a power he has because he's part demon. They're called paramortals because they're not quite mortal but not celestial either. Paramortals have different powers so it's hard to know what they'll be like before you meet them since their power usually reflects a deep desire. But across the board, most of them can blend in and avoid attracting attention from outsiders. People don't remember encounters they've had with paramortals even if it's something significant that they wouldn't be able to forget about ordinarily. It's like the woman with the car."

"The what?"

"See? Think back to this morning. What happened while you were running today?"

Casey fell silent to think, finding it true. A large section of her morning was hazy. Until One had reminded her, she had forgotten that most of it had happened at all. Grabbing the wheel, the car crash, the body on the ground, seeing all that blood coating One's hands, all of it was foggy and she had to work to recall any of it. "Am I going to forget about it all the way?"

"Most likely. You'll forget about the man too. It's the same thing that happened with everyone here. Especially since they weren't involved, they barely even registered the trader when he grabbed you and they certainly don't remember him now."

An intrusive thought poked its way into Casey's mind and she pushed closer to One, interlocking their arms. "Does that rule apply to all paramortals or just the demon kind? Because if you're half angel... Am I going to forget about you too?"

One was silent for the length of a breath. "Think about it. I bought us train tickets. You went through my pockets and I'm not carrying any money. The guy who sold me two tickets for nothing has no idea he did it. It's not something you need to worry about though. This will be over soon and you won't remember and it won't matter by then."

Biting her lip, Casey rested her head on One's shoulder. She didn't think she could get any more obvious, but One wasn't picking up her hints. She didn't want to forget about him. Safe or threatened, Casey didn't want to leave One's side again for any reason.

XIII

ONE

Surprise threatened to rise to the surface of One's expression. Half-angel? That hadn't been part of any lie or incomplete truth One had told so far. Acacia had mentioned it, but One hadn't thought she'd held onto that theory. He had to admit, it did make sense for her to reach that conclusion if she thought One was really on her side and it was probably making the job a lot easier.

It was funny how much she seemed to care. The jobs One used to work in soul trade had never turned out like this. One had always been a fan of ruses to trap his targets rather than brute strength, but he'd never had one trust him so fully like this. Watching Acacia out of the corner of his eye, she seemed comfortable leaning against One. With the memory of the most recent trader already fading, she didn't look nervous at all. She trusted One.

And it was the worst mistake she could've ever made.

One wondered if other soul traders charmed their victims

into coming with them like this. One didn't see himself as particularly charming, but maybe it was Acacia who was different. It was possible it had something to do with her own role in saving herself from the other traders. When One had regularly worked in soul trade, he had always done all the work and rarely needed any help from the victim. This time around, Acacia had helped get herself away from the woman by crashing the car and escaping up the ladder while One distracted the man. She trusted One because he trusted her. Instead of One holding all the power, this was closer to teamwork. As long as Acacia believed they were still on the same side of the battle, she would be drawn closer. One hoped that wouldn't cause unforeseen problems when handing her over to Gogmuth.

Tracing her hand up One's arm, Acacia pressed closer. "Are you mad at me?"

"No."

"I almost let your knife thing get taken and you risked yourself for me again."

"Risking myself is my job. And getting captured wasn't your fault; I shouldn't have dropped my guard. And I got my nail back so don't worry about it."

"Why do you fight with a nail?" Acacia sat up straight, pulling away to look at One more directly instead of leaning against him.

Pulling the crucifix nail out into the open, One slid a finger down the edge of it, careful not to press too hard. He wondered how much he could tell Acacia without ruining her image of him. "It's a holy nail. There are only three in existence. This nail held Christ to the cross."

Acacia's eyes widened. "How is it still in one piece? It should've disintegrated by now, but you use it like a dagger."

"It has powers." As easy as it was for One to say that, living in a world full of inhuman abilities, he knew this would be mind-blowing for Acacia. "Things that came into contact with Christ have immense strength, especially against demons. A hit from a holy nail will kill a demon without question. It's pretty dangerous for humans and paramortals as well so I'd advise you don't mess with it again."

"Sorry..." Acacia sat straight in the seat, fingering the pocket of her hoodie shirt. "I was nervous and I didn't know if I could trust you and you were sleeping..."

"I probably would've done the same." One shrugged, glancing out the window at the approaching city. Knowing it was Acacia who had gone through his pockets gave One a little more hope that the demon blood wasn't lost forever with the trader. "Do you still have the other thing you took from me or did you lose it in the fight?"

Acacia dipped into her pocket and drew out the glass vial, looking relieved to be handing it back.

Waking up with no demon blood, One had almost resigned himself to death on the spot, but having the last few precious doses safe in his hand again renewed what little hope he had left for succeeding in this assignment. One couldn't blame Acacia for taking the unknown substance either. Had he been in her shoes, One was sure he would've done the same thing. The consequences of nearly losing his prized weapon and last bit of demon blood were One's to shoulder alone. Falling asleep had been a huge mistake and he knew to come out of the situation unscathed with the nail, the demon blood, and Acacia was extremely lucky. It made One skeptical of how long the luck was going to last.

"What is it?" Acacia finally blurted the obvious question, innocent brown eyes reflecting her hesitation. She might trust One, but the tube of dark liquid looked menacing by anyone's standards.

"Something you don't need to know about," One said, stuffing it back into the pocket of his white vest. There was no way to explain it and keep Acacia's trust without lying and something still held One back from that simple action. "Thank you for not losing it. I apologize for falling asleep and not looking after you better. That's my bad."

"Are you okay?" Acacia couldn't sit still in the bench seat, now sideways and resting a hand on One's knee. "I don't know if this is what you're always like, but I worry about you sometimes. You look like you're not happy or you don't feel good. Are you sick?"

It wasn't a false statement. Withdrawal from reduced

demon blood intake sapped One's energy and left him feeling hollow. He figured he probably looked the part, tired and wasted. One patted his pocket, hoping Acacia would interpret to mean the vial was medicine. "You could say that. It's not something a mortal can catch though so don't worry about it."

"You have to drink *that*?" Acacia bit her lip like she wanted to say something else, but sat back against the seat instead, leaning her head against the glass window pane as the train pulled them into the heart of the city. She had no idea she was calmly riding toward a personal tragedy. If she knew what was waiting for her only a half-mile of crowded city blocks away, if she knew who One was, she wouldn't be daydreaming out the window, she wouldn't be running to One for comfort or to be held.

It didn't matter what One thought of her either. Once she was delivered to Gogmuth's hands, One wouldn't see her again, wouldn't know what happened to her. The job would be done and he would be paid and there would be no use in thinking about her, but One hoped in a hidden part of his heart that she might get lucky.

XIV

CASEY

Stepping off the train with One, Casey couldn't shake an intrusive thought that had barged into her mind near the end of the ride. For an instant, she had felt safe again, when the trader made of metal had died and she had stood in the empty back of the train car with One's arms around her, but the paranoia was back. One's suspicions about the third potential trader had stuck with her and every single stranger milling about the train station was now a threat to her. She wanted to believe that she'd be safe once she got to One's destination, but any sort of security felt like an illusion after the day she'd had, if it had ever really existed.

By the way his eyes never stopped moving, inspecting the city, One was probably thinking the same thing so Casey didn't bother relaying her fears to her escort. Thinking about One made Casey feel guilty. In the grand scheme of things, Casey was utterly useless to him — worse than useless, she was slowing One down, putting him in danger. She rarely needed saving from anyone and it was an unusual sensation for her. Of the people she was closest to, Casey thought she might be the one doing most of the saving. Dylan was a great boyfriend and she didn't mind doting on him to make sure he felt affirmed. Rose would drop everything to save Casey if needed, but the need had never really arisen before. Even in her family, Casey didn't know if any of them had needed to intervene in her life before to set her back on the right path. Picturing her other relationships, Casey realized she hadn't even stopped long enough to miss home yet today.

The reality of the situation was that she needed to be saved now and a rescuer had been put in place for her. Casey's heart tightened in her chest like it had on the train when she'd been taken captive. Blinking at the ground, Casey sent up a quick prayer, thanking God for keeping her safe. It had occurred to her in the heart of danger that she didn't need to be in a church to pray, thank God, or ask for His hand of protection. She could do that wherever she was and she wanted to do it more often. She had a lot to be grateful for, especially after the reminder of all she had to lose.[13]

Casey looked up at her companion, unable to express her gratitude in words and watching it fade in a twinge of guilt. One had saved her already from two traders while she had been helpless to keep from being kidnapped, practically inviting danger. One's expression was strained and unhappy. Knowing he was sick didn't even surprise Casey now that she knew. One seemed sure of himself, but Casey could feel the ghost of strength underneath One's movements. He was only a shell of who he could be. He was weakened by whatever angel disease he had and he still put everything into defending Casey. Maybe at some point, Casey would get the chance to save One someday too and she would stop feeling so guilty.

Biting her lip, Casey slid a hand into One's, hoping the coolness of his skin would calm her racing pulse and aching heart. "I tried to fight back."

One barely glanced at her, focused elsewhere. "Hm?"

Casey felt her eyes fill with angry tears. She hated crying in front of other people and it felt like she'd spent all day crying in front of One. She stopped walking and yanked on One's hand, forcing him to stop as well. "I'm sorry for being such a burden on you! I'm sorry you have to keep saving me and even then, I act like I don't trust you and I take the only weapon you have and make it harder for you to fight. I really tried to get away from the guy on the train, okay? I tried cutting his arm with the nail, but it barely fazed him. Even when I try, I'm not as strong as you. You say you're sick and I don't know what that medicine is or what it's doing for you, but I'm worried and I feel awful that you have to keep rescuing me when you should be rescuing yourself. I know I'm not special to you because you barely look at me, but you're really important to me. You probably do this all the time for people but I'm not used to being helpless while you're so strong and I'm worried about you because I care about you, One. You act like you're the only person in the world who can do any saving and you have to look out for yourself and everyone else because you can't rely on me and I understand that because I'm useless, but I want you to trust me like I trust you!"

The air around them disappeared into a vacuum. Breathless, Casey tipped her head back to look into One's eyes. The magic and mystique she was falling in love with glittered like ice, bright in the midday sunlight.

One slid his hand out of Casey's and turned away. "May I take you to get something to eat, Acacia?"

The calm response extinguished the inferno in Casey's heart. She wanted to be furious. How dare One keep that straight expression when her entire world was falling apart? How dare he suggest a lunch date when their lives were on the line? Yet, Casey couldn't find it in her to be mad. She followed obediently. "You don't have to pretend to be nice to me because I yelled at you."

Instead of responding right away, One led Casey into a large building with restaurants and snack bars, selecting one at random and standing in line to order. "What would you like?"

Casey selected a sandwich off the overhead menu.

"Stay close." One moved toward the counter, ordering, receiving the sandwich, and moving away again without paying.

"I'm never going to understand how you do that..." Casey

took the sandwich from One's hands, her expression betraying her fascination. She was about to prompt a discussion of the questions she'd asked before, calmer now than in the heat of her explosion, but One started walking again and she ran to catch up.

The white-haired stranger never looked at her but started to explain anyway. "We need to move quickly. Sorry we don't have time to sit down and eat, but you should keep your strength up. Keep an eye out for anyone who seems to be tailing us. I went the long way through the food court, but someone could still be tracking us. I'm sorry for being curt with you, but I don't think you're helpless. I don't think I've met a mortal who would've crashed that car or escaped out the back of the train or tried to use the nail. It's not your fault that didn't work either. The trader's powers probably kept him safe from being cut so it wouldn't have worked if I tried either. I make a lot of assumptions about the weakness of humans, but you've taught me otherwise. You're resourceful and you've been invaluable in helping me."

Casey struggled to keep up with One's brisk pace while processing all the new information. She stared down at her sandwich. "You're not going to eat something?"

One sighed, but it didn't sound as cold as his tone usually was. "Again, is that really the most pressing question you have?"

Laughing, Casey bit into her lunch. The half-smile in One's

voice was enough to satisfy any follow-up questions she could've thought up.

After skipping breakfast, the sandwich was extra wonderful. She glanced from side to side, mapping her surroundings without moving her head to give away where she was looking, the way One did. She didn't see anyone who appeared to be following them, but there were too many people in the downtown square to watch at once.

Something small and black on the pavement caught Casey's eye and she slowed down to look at it, then stopped and stumbled away from it. "One? That's my phone. I lost it this morning in that lady's car."

Before she could reach out to retrieve it, One's hand appeared on her shoulder, pulling her away. "Don't touch that, Acacia. Think. How did that get here?"

The day's perils were far from over. Out of the corner of her eye, Casey spotted something faster than the rest of the people on the plaza, a small black terrier dog, dragging a leash behind it. The dog was looking right at her and Casey felt dread like she had never known before. The morning had become fuzzy and the train ride was starting to follow suit, but Casey remembered the first moment she had started believing in the danger around her.

When she'd first met the woman while running from One, she had been walking a dog. Casey had climbed into a car she was positive hadn't been parked on the curb before. The gray-haired woman started the car and Casey had looked around for where the little dog had gone but the car had already started moving and Casey was trapped.

Casey felt frozen with ice in her veins as she pointed at the dog. "That belonged to the lady you killed this morning. Why is it here?"

Eyes narrowing, One spotted the dog too, backing slowly away from it, even though it was all the way across the plaza.

Fear radiated off One's sweater and landed on Casey, tying her stomach into knots as she watched the little dog shift and stand up, transforming into a woman in her twenties, tall and lithe. Her long, black hair tumbled down her shoulders, blending with a slim, black dress. Black heels struck pavement and Casey thought she could hear each step the woman took in their direction.

"Run, Acacia." A cold hand slid into Casey's but she barely registered it, even as she was pulled from her spot on the concrete to sprint away from the woman.

XV

ONE

Shapeshifter.

The question of the third trader's identity had plagued One all day, but the answer sent chills down his spine. There was no more mystery to the method of the third trader or how she had managed to stay completely out of sight for the entire day.

For a moment, One was dragging Acacia behind him, away from the plaza, then she was running on her own, easily keeping up with One, even taking the lead until she didn't know where they were running to.

The only option now was to hope they got to Gogmuth's designated drop-off point before the shapeshifting trader caught up to them. They didn't have any sort of advantage since the third trader knew the location as well as One did. But as much as One hated the reality of the situation, there was no way he would be able to fight off a paramortal with so much power. Even Acacia had noticed that One's strength was waning so the last trader had probably seen the weakness from the beginning. It made sense for her to wait in the shadows, disguised, and let One do all the dirty work of killing the other traders and bringing Acacia downtown. The trader would wait until One had run out of strength to fight and then she would strike.

It was probably going to work.

One motioned for Acacia to follow him, dashing down a street, elbowing pedestrians out of the way, none of them looking more than slightly inconvenienced with the disturbance, cloaked by the powers of One's paramortality.

"Where are we going?" Acacia yelled, breathing hard but keeping pace easily.

"Drop off point."

Concern creased Acacia's brow. "Drop what off? What about the safe house?"

"Just follow me!" One didn't have time or focus enough to enhance the ruse anymore. He was leading Acacia to her demise and it wouldn't be long before she found out the truth anyway, that One wasn't on her side, that no guardian angel had been sent to protect her, that she was being handed over to Gogmuth and there was no hope of escape. The only uncertainty was whether the final delivery would be made by One or the shapeshifting trader.

Without bothering to look over his shoulder, One pounded the sidewalk until they reached the destination.

The drop-off point was inside a large warehouse, brick like

most of the older city structures and unused for any other purposes. It operated under the same kind of magic that the paramortals did, blending in so well with the surrounding city that nobody else could see it. Even guided by One, Acacia almost missed the entrance, not designed to be seen by mortal eyes.

One took her by the shoulders and led her inside, risking a glance at the street they'd come from. There was no sign of the trader, but that was more likely bad news than good. One refused to believe they had lost her. It was much more likely that she would be waiting for them, hidden in plain sight somewhere.

The prospect of succeeding with the delivery had been an optimistic dream in One's head earlier in the day. Now he didn't know why he'd ever believed it was possible at all.

Upon entering the building, One knew something was off. The warehouse was one large room, split up by a few support columns. In the center of the concrete floor, a large pentagram was drawn with precisely scripted runes. Most large cities had a secret building intended for the delivery of human souls to the demons that commissioned them.

One had seen the insides of trade houses plenty of times in the past and they always felt *prepared* to receive the human offering. There was a hunger in the air, emanating from the pentagram, like the awaiting demon was trapped just beneath the concrete floor, ready for its next meal.

This trade house lacked the unrestrained pull for human flesh. The pentagram in the center of the floor looked normal, but it was dead, One was positive. If he had all the time and demon blood in the world, he would jump back into his home realm and use his own pentagram to get in contact with Gogmuth, making sure the bounty was still good. Unfortunately, One had neither of those luxuries and there was little else to do than keep going and see what happened.

Acacia turned around to look at One, eyes blown wide with fear. "One, what is that? What is this place?"

One was saved the betrayal of the next step: twisting Acacia's arms behind her back and leading her to the star design in the floor to complete the transaction. Before he could move, something cold and smooth wrapped around his neck, like his scarf had come to life to choke him. From the rafters above the entrance, a jet black snake dipped its head down to hiss a laugh in One's face, another section of the body squeezing tighter around One's throat.

Clasping her hands over her mouth, Acacia fell backward and stifled a scream, tears wetting her cheeks again. "Let go of One!" she yelled, backing away from the snake.

Another hissy chuckle escaped the snake's mouth. One kept still but could feel the long body creep over his shoulders and run a loop around his chest. A single wrong move meant the shapeshifter would constrict One's life away in less time than a heart's final beat.

"Let go of One!" Acacia screeched again. "You bitch, let him go!"

"I can't believe you kept up the lie this long, One," the snake said, sounding very amused and all too pleased with herself. "She still believes you're on her side. That's impressive, especially for someone like you. Acacia, darling, I'm afraid not everything here is as it seems."

Dark eyes flicking between One and the snake, Acacia stopped crying. "What does she mean, One? If she's trying to tell me I can't trust you, it's okay; I don't believe her." The teenager faltered, visibly terrified. "I know what you are! You're part-demon, paramortal. You were the dog I saw this morning with the first lady who tried to take me then you shapeshifted into the car she used to drive away. Were you partners? I know you want to capture me and take me to a demon, but One isn't going to let that happen!"

Acacia's voice cracked, not unnoticed by One. He focused on an escape plan instead. One didn't have a lot of experience with shapeshifters, but he wondered if the trader had sustained damage from being run into a light pole as a car, if there was a chink in the snake's armor One could use to get free if he could grab the crucifix nail from his pocket.

The serpent took her time laughing at Acacia before responding. "You know a lot, little mortal. I hope that doesn't cause you unnecessary problems when you meet Gogmuth. He doesn't like when humans know too much about celestials and their agenda. Unfortunately, I don't believe you'll be escaping this. One isn't your conventional soul trader or I expect we would've met in the field before, but he shares the same goal that I do. There's a very pretty bounty on your head, Acacia Wickstrom, and both of us want it."

"You're lying!" a defiant fire smoldered in Acacia's eyes. "I'll never believe the words of a half-demon!"

"You should take your own advice," the trader chuckled, constricting around One's chest. "I'm not surprised though. A little girl will always trust a pretty face."

Doubt snuck onto Acacia's expression and she approached One cautiously. Delicately avoiding touching the snake, Acacia fingered the pocket of One's white vest, drawing out the vial of demon blood, letting it catch the light. "You told me you were an angel..."

"I never said that," One sighed. The snake uncurled from around his neck to let him speak. The trader was delighted to let the drama play out now that there was no risk to her bounty. Watching Acacia's world crumble while One struggled to take each breath was the height of entertainment for a soul trader. One sipped in another shallow breath. "Acacia, you told yourself that and I didn't correct you. Half-angels don't exist. Angels don't pawn their blood off to humans the way demons do."

The hurt on Acacia's face was painful to look at. One closed his eyes and wished for death. A faint crash drew his gaze up again, finding Acacia's face twisted into a betrayed frown. At her feet lay shattered glass and a tiny black puddle of the last few doses of One's demon blood.

XVI

CASEY

The entire day had held terror after terror but the sight of the black snake dangling from the ceiling, wrapped around One was the worst of all. Casey hated every word the serpent spoke against One, but her companion wasn't arguing, wasn't trying to defend himself. One's dark eyes were dull, searching the floor, giving in, admitting the ugly truth. The only thing that set One apart from the other traders was his success in tricking Casey. And she'd believed every word he said, fooled into caring about him, enjoying the feeling of his hand in hers, appreciating his quirks, worrying about his apparent sickness. One wasn't sick; he was a demon.

Casey smashed the vial on the ground, unsure of why. It didn't undo the damage done, didn't put her back home, didn't erase the betrayal. Inexplicably, Casey was angrier at the demon blood itself than at One. Maybe it was all part of the ruse, but One had saved her from worse fates with the other traders and he had bought her lunch and had let her cling and even smiled back once.

The snake looked elated. "That's all you had left, treasure hunter? How long have you been rationing demon blood? You must have one foot in the grave already. Honestly, it almost makes me sad. You did well against the other traders for being so weak and I should've like to fight you at full strength."

One kept his eyes fixed on the ground, never looking at the snake. "Acacia, run far away from here and don't look back. I'm not trying to trick you this time."

"How sweet!" The serpent crooned, nudging One's cheek with her long scaly body. "You're not going anywhere but hell; there's no use trying to redeem yourself at the end."

"I know—" One choked as the snake constricted. "I know where I'm going. Acacia, you don't have to end up there too. So run."

Casey stood frozen as she met One's blue eyes, pleading, begging her to listen. The feeling of betrayal escaped Casey's chest and left her feeling hollow. She should've felt satisfied knowing One was going to die for tricking her, but she couldn't even run away knowing it would mean breaking the eye contact she held with her enemy who pretended to be her guardian angel.

"Uh oh," the snake teased. "She's not as smart as you think she is. Even after all this, she's still loyal to the weakest paramortal of all time."

"Just... kill me already." One broke the eye contact,

obviously struggling to keep breathing.

"Oh, I could." The serpent's head poked closer to One's, tongue flicking in and out. "Or I could leave you a little longer to watch since you seem to care so much about Acacia and what happens to her. I could let you watch Gogmuth kill her, destroy her mind or turn her into one of us. I could even start that myself. I'd let you watch me bite her." Fangs glistened in the low light.

One writhed in the snake's grip, eyes widening. "You know you can't give demon blood to a mortal. That's against soul trade code."

"Maybe Gogmuth would thank me for starting the process. Like you said, she's resourceful. Demons don't like difficult prey. They'd rather recruit the smart ones."

Gasping for breath, One struggled to speak forcefully. "Acacia, you're not going to get another chance. You need to go."

Strangely, the most remorse Casey felt was that she hadn't been able to repay the favor and save One like she had wanted to. Maybe trying to save herself would be good enough. Casey whirled around and sprinted through the building to look for a way out. She avoided the center of the room and the pentagram, apparently her real destination all along.

A noise behind her made Casey put on a burst of speed like she was running track, hearing telltale footsteps of someone trying to catch up with her. She didn't get far before arms locked around her, strong, human arms, the snake guise gone. Casey twisted and screamed, catching glimpses of the black-haired woman behind her, looking smug and victorious.

Sobs broke free of Casey's chest as she was dragged toward the pentagram in the center of the building. The trader whispered in her ear. "No need to get upset, darling. If you're lucky, you won't remember any of this and you can live your life again the way you did before. Everything will be in order with your soul and no one will have to trick you or take you again."

Casey whipped her head around, looking for a sign of One. He wasn't by the door anymore. She didn't know where he could've gone or if he had even survived after Casey shattered the moment of strained peace by running away.

The toe of Casey's shoe touched the edge of the pentagram and immediately, she felt the power rush through her. It was a dark, ominous power that she knew instinctively to fear. The trader stepped fully into the circle, pulling Casey along with her. In a flash of white and black, Casey spotted One, sprinting toward her, poised to tackle with his jaw squared and his eyes locked on target.

Time stopped for a moment, allowing Casey to feel a lot of things at once. She almost smiled at One, still relentlessly trying to get her back, but there was grief under the surface, knowing it was too late to be saved. She was already within the pentagram and energy built like static electricity until a blinding flash blew her away from the trader, her mind going dark.

XVII

ONE

Smoke tickled the inside of One's nose. The trade house was on fire. This wasn't what was supposed to happen.

One toed the edge of the pentagram as the deafening crack of lightning struck the center of the room and he was sent skidding backward across the concrete, burning pain in his chest.

Confusion only registered for a moment before One knew what had happened. The daily risk of working for demons had nothing on the danger of standing on Holy War battleground. Gogmuth was not waiting on the other side of the pentagram and the link to the demon world had been severed. The hot bolt of light was no demon trick; it was the work of an angel.[14]

Something had gone very wrong recently and it had left the building rigged to blow as soon as someone stepped into the pentagram. Somehow, the heavens had learned about the deal going down, kicked the demon out, and intervened.

It explained the burning in One's chest as well. Angelic

traps were simple in purpose that way. Anyone demonic in nature who touched the trap — the pentagram in this case — would be eliminated. Angel traps were extremely effective in wiping out demons and paramortals, veins swimming with demon blood.

For the first time, One's shortage of demon blood may have actually been a blessing. Every molecule of the poison inside his body was caught on holy fire, burning away to leave One a rapidly dying husk of what he had been, but still alive as it took longer to target the demonic traces in his bloodstream. It looked like the shapeshifting trader had not met the same kind fate, her lean, feminine body crumpled on the floor, unmoving, a short distance away from the pentagram. Surely, she had been full of demon blood and the angel trap would have destroyed her almost instantly.

One spotted Acacia too, moving around easily. Fully mortal, the blast wouldn't have done more than stun her. The dark-haired teen was moving toward the trader, kneeling next to the body.

Anxious to get back to her, One got to his knees. Immediately, he vomited on the ground, mostly dark red blood. The demonic essence inside of One wasn't going to burn quietly; it was going to take One down with it. Paramortals weren't supposed to return to mortality.

Pushing through the pain, One stumbled in Acacia's direction. Safety was still a far-off illusion and setting off an angel trap was never over quickly. The warriors of heaven would come running to make sure their prey was dead and the demon realm would be furious at the destruction of a trade house and leap into action as well. In seconds, this entire building would be swarming with angels and demons both and no one was safe in the middle of the Holy War, mortal or immortal.

The safest place, of course, would be to retreat into One's home realm, but there was no guarantee the dimension would even hold together with One on death's doorstep. Even if he got there, escape was near impossible. But it might still be better than dying here today and going straight to hell.

A wall caved in on the far side of the room, letting in a blinding light. Angels. The floor rumbled and the concrete cracked, hissing snarls trailing up from below. Demons.

One broke forward at a sprint, a scream breaking past his mouth for the corroding, burning demon blood left inside him, praying it would last just long enough. Holding an arm out, One raced toward Acacia. The girl was on her knees, looking terrified at the entrance of the angels. She could go blind in milliseconds from looking directly at them and that was only if a rift in the floor didn't send her falling straight down to Hell first.

One snatched her, holding her against his chest, and ceased to exist on Earth.

Part 2

XVIII

CASEY

Casey wasn't sure what it was supposed to feel like to be taken by a demon but she didn't think the spike of light, heat, and energy in the warehouse was it. The first clue was that the shapeshifting trader was dead across the room; Casey didn't think demons could afford to kill their employees before delivering a bounty.

Getting to her feet and shaking off some of the dizziness, Casey found herself on the opposite side of the room from where she started and spotted One, closer to the entrance, also blown back by the blast but still moving. Casey could feel her heart screaming to run back to One's side, the place she'd felt safest all day. Together, they could find a way out, even as the building shook around her like it was being lifted from the Earth. Then reality crashed back down and Casey reminded herself she couldn't trust One and not even this odd explosion reconciled the fact that they stood on different sides of the battlefield.

Maybe, Casey reasoned with herself, One could be useful to her in other ways if she played her cards right. At least, that could be the excuse she used to justify sticking around the white-haired paramortal. Casey found herself split with her brain saying 'no' while her heart pleaded 'yes' and drove her forward, back toward the center of the room instead of away toward an exit.

In order to have some control over One, Casey needed leverage, something he needed: demon blood, obviously. One had carried it in his jacket to use when needed so Casey assumed the other trader might be playing a similar hand. Only stumbling once, Casey knelt by the woman, overcome with a wave of emotions — mostly sickness and fear. Before this morning, she had never seen a real dead body and now she had seen three and she was touching the last, slipping a hand into a zippered pocket of the woman's dress. In the back of Casey's mind, she expected the woman's eyes to pop open as she lunged forward to kill Casey like a horror movie, but the body lay still as Casey drew out four vials, each one full of black liquid.

A wall of the building crumbled and the floor started to crack apart but Casey ignored it, running a speech through her head of the deal she was going to make with One, how she held his last hope of survival in her hands. Even if they could never be partners again like they had been that morning, at least Casey could pretend she was helping repay the favor to save

One's life.

Casey turned away from the light that hurt her head even without looking at it. She was met with torn black jeans and cold hands outstretched for her as the warehouse completely vanished.

Casey opened her eyes to a sight no less confusing. Flat on her back, Casey found a white ceiling above her, bare aside from a small light, turned off as sunlight cast the shape of windows onto the walls. The walls were warm beige and featured a display of framed pictures. The floor beneath Casey was dark hardwood, but she could barely tell for all the gold and silver coins, chains, and miscellanea strewn across the surface. Sitting up, Casey analyzed all sides of her silent, alien surroundings. The white inside of a front door met her head on as if she'd fallen through it to get here. Beside her, Casey used the back of a brown leather couch to get to her feet, looking over it into a cozy living room complete with another couch, a TV, and a coffee table. The table held a few empty glasses and plates while jewels and more gold spilled onto the floor.

Aside from the treasure, Casey seemed to have landed in the entryway of a simple family home. The floor was solid under her feet, the only proof Casey had that she wasn't dreaming. The air was incredibly warm and she found herself sweating in moments even though she was already clothed for running and summer weather.

Casey leaned back against the door, placing her left hand on the wall and her right on the arm of the couch, hoping to steady the dizziness. Ahead of her was a short hallway and a glimpse of a kitchen table where it opened up. On the floor next to a table, One lay face-down, unmoving, sprawled awkwardly on the wood floor, a few random precious metal objects around him.

Taking a shaky step forward, Casey moved down the hall toward him and quickly found the hallway elongating before her eyes. With each step she took toward One, the further she was from him. Then the path suddenly ended in an invisible wall and she could only go left or right even though One still appeared to be right in front of her.

The maze laid out around Casey didn't make sense according to any law of physics Casey was familiar with. Feeling like crying again, Casey pounded on the barrier that kept her from going straight. Déjà vu reminded her of the morning's events when the street signs around her home had led her in circles around the neighborhood and more pieces of the puzzle clicked into place. She figured she really ought to be finding an escape plan, rather than persistently moving toward One and his deceptions and traps. Running senselessly hadn't helped that morning either, but Casey took off down the right-hand hallway, following wherever it led her, down a flight of stairs, onto a backyard porch overlooking a dramatic sunset, under a trellis, back inside a minimalistic home office. With increasing frustration, Casey followed the corridors of the funhouse from room to room, all in strange position in relation to one another, gravity changing directions sometimes as she walked on the ceiling of a bathroom and had to crawl through the doorway into a dining room. Casey's feet touched the floor solidly in that room and she was relieved. A table of light colored wood stretched from end to end of the dining room, set with four places, blocking Casey from the only other way out of the room, a large window set into the far wall. She felt like she had been running for hours though she hadn't managed to escape the small house and she had no idea where she was in relation to either the front door or One.

With some difficulty, Casey crossed the room, crawling under the table and slipping through the window into whatever she would find next.

The window was now the ceiling and Casey fell through it onto the floor of a carpeted room, once again landing hard on her back.

Wincing, Casey sat up only to have her breath catch in her chest.

Toy train in hand, a boy no older than ten stood on a bed, eyeing Casey with wonder. "Hello? Are you Acacia? One mentioned you. I didn't think he was going to bring you here though."

Casey sat up slowly, hesitant to trust anything in the mixed up house. Any second, one of the light blue walls would become the floor and she'd start sliding or the ground would drop out from under her and she'd fall into the attic. The boy would turn out to be a figment of her imagination or some sort of monster in disguise.

The boy bounced once on the mattress before putting his train down and hopping down to the floor. He had medium-toned skin, pine-green eyes, and brown hair a shade lighter than Casey's. His small hands were childlike and plump and he waved to Casey. "Hello? Can you talk?"

"Um, yeah..." Casey brushed hair out of her eyes, baffled by the small child. "Who are you?"

A white smile lit up the boy's face, gapped where he'd lost one of his baby teeth that hadn't grown in yet. "You are Acacia, aren't you! I didn't think I was going to get to meet you! I'm One's little brother; my name is Ezra Valera! You're going to help One, right?"

"Help One with what?"

The smile dropped off Ezra's face. "Haven't you seen what the house is doing? One said he would be able to fix it but he hasn't yet and I'm getting scared. I don't even want to go out there because I might get lost."

The little boy's eyes filled with tears and Casey rushed forward to comfort him. Instead, her hand passed through Ezra like a ghost would and she shrank back. Ezra didn't seem to notice and threw his arms around Casey's neck, as solid as anything else. Casey tried not to show her shock as she patted

Ezra's back. "It's okay, I'm sure there's a way to fix this, don't you think? I'll find One and he'll know what to do."

"Be careful," Ezra whispered in her ear. "I think something's wrong with One. He's been acting weird for a long time and when I ask, he says it's nothing. That means he thinks I'm too little to understand, but maybe you can find out. One's been back a few times and he never stays for long, but it sounds like he trusts you."

Listening to the raw pain in Ezra's voice made Casey's chest feel tight. Taking Ezra at face value, he had no idea what One was, what he did for a living, that he was a bad guy. Yet it opened up another facet of One's identity Casey hadn't seen before. He'd kidnapped her, tried to trade her in for more demon blood, he was unfriendly and talked down to Casey. But he had a kind side too and Ezra fit like a puzzle piece into that side of the story, an innocent bystander who looked up to One like he was his everything.

Casey wanted to ask Ezra to come with her, hesitating at the last second. Between the two of them, they might be able to cover more ground, but what they found might not be pleasant. Lying on the kitchen floor, One was unconscious at best and dead at worst and Casey would never dream of making Ezra witness his dead brother if the worst case scenario came true.

Casey stood up, offering an encouraging smile to Ezra. "I'll find One and we'll all work this out, okay?" She almost reached out to touch Ezra again, but withdrew, unsure if her hand would pass through him again, then left through the bedroom door.

Stepping through the doorway, Casey found herself in the front entryway again, the knob of the front door still in her hand. She turned around, half expecting to see back into Ezra's bedroom, but instead saw the front porch as if the house had finally righted itself. Casey glanced over her shoulder and saw One's limp form still in the kitchen. But was he really her responsibility? Was any of this? She should be focused on escape and it was right here in front of her.

It felt funny to step back through the door she'd come from, but Casey stepped back through the front door. But instead of the porch, the house had other plans for her. Shuffling her feet as her eyes got wider, Casey found herself standing in a field of tall, green grass that brushed her legs gently as it swayed in the breeze. On the horizon, the sun was dipping lower in the sky, lighting everything on golden fire.

Casey turned a full circle, shock setting in. How had she gone suddenly from inside the house to the middle of a field? She held her hands out, feeling through the air, but finding no link back to the bedroom or the entryway or anything else. Squinting into the sunlight, Casey spotted a house, hopefully, the one she'd come from. Though it made no sense, Casey ran back toward it, praying she could get in and have another chance to find One even if the world around her kept trying to keep them apart.

Hands on the front door again, Casey took a deep breath and stepped back inside, relieved to find everything the way it had looked when she woke up in the foyer. The gold coins still littered the floor so not everything was in order, but at least she was back where she started. Cautious, Casey walked into the kitchen, the hallway now functioning as it was supposed to. It was almost creepier now that everything was seemingly normal.

Casey knelt down by One's still form, holding her breath. She set her fingers against her companion's neck, flinching at how cold his skin was. From anyone else, Casey would assume the worst, but One was always this cold. Weak as it was, Casey could feel his pulse and she exhaled in relief. She still didn't know what to do or how to fix the house or help Ezra or deal with One, but at least he was alive.

A noise like a cough across the room caught Casey's attention and her head jerked up. She found herself staring into her own eyes. An entire wall of the kitchen had become a mirror, though Casey didn't assume for a second that it was supposed to be that way. The house wasn't done trapping her in its maze.

Staring into the reflection, Casey heard another weak cough and watched One stir under her hand. She looked down in surprise, but the One she was really touching hadn't moved.

More than a little skeptical, Casey stood up and approached the mirror, her reflection coming to meet her like it was supposed to. She touched hands with her reflection and felt herself slip through the mirror, stumbling into a kitchen identical to the original, but backward. Casey turned, eyeing herself from the opposite side of the mirror. A louder cough beckoned her further into the mirror world, kneeling by One's body as his shoulders tensed and he shifted, blinking hazy blue eyes up at her.

Before Casey could decide what to do, One sat up, touching her hand. "Acacia?"

"U-um," Casey stammered. "Are you okay? I was really worried. I thought you were dead."

"Well, I don't think I'm dead," One said dryly, running a hand through his white hair. "Are you okay? Sorry for dragging you here with me, but the trade house isn't safe. There's probably still a Holy War battle going on there as we speak and I couldn't leave you there to get killed."

Casey smiled as she started to relax. One didn't let go of his serious expression, even though they were both safe here. "It's okay. Thank you for rescuing me."

One smiled back like he was hesitant to let it be seen. He leaned toward Casey. "You saved me first. Thanks."

The *warmth* in One's voice was hard to believe, but it brightened Casey's smile even more. "So what is this place?"

"It's a separate realm from Earth. I live here. It's not usually like this, so broken and crazy. I think I should be able to fix it though. Well, most of it. You tried going out the front door, didn't you? And it didn't work?"

Casey shook her head. "Not really, it spat me out in the middle of a field but I found my way back. Is that bad?"

"Yeah." One looked down. "I'll do what I can but I don't know if we're going to be able to escape here. Although... I'm okay with that if you are."

Heart slamming in her chest, Casey realized that she was touching One, leaning into him and he was leaning into her, unlike on the train when One had sat stiffly while Casey did her best to make her affection known. She slid her fingers between One's hoping her expression didn't betray everything happening in her heart. The real world tried to impress upon her for a moment, but Casey pushed it away. She'd even dated a couple guys before finding Dylan, but none of them made her feel so alive like this.

One closed the distance between them, kissing Casey with gentle lips, dry but not chapped, cool but not cold.

Casey pushed herself closer against One, giving in to the sensation of the kiss, so unlike anything she'd experienced before. Pulling away to take a breath, One stared into her eyes with an intensity that made her blush and look away.

Out of the corner of her eye, Casey spotted the mirror again and it froze her in place. The One on the other side of the glass was still lying motionless on the floor while the other

Casey knelt over him with a hand on his back, looking at the mirror with hopelessness in her eyes. Casey pulled away as this One tried to kiss her again.

"Acacia. What's wrong?"

"C-can you see that?" Casey motioned to the mirror.

"You don't need to worry about it. I've got you."

Casey allowed herself to be pulled tighter against One's body and she couldn't deny how good it felt — but it was unnatural. The One she knew wouldn't willingly have his hands all over her. As much as it hurt to admit, he didn't love her that way. "What is it then? Why are there two of us?"

"It's like two different realities," One explained patiently, playing with Casey's dark curls.

Pulling away, Casey stared at her One. "So in that reality, you might still be dying, but in this reality, you actually love me?"

One laughed, a gentle noise that was just as pleasant yet jarringly out of place as the kiss was. "It's what you want, isn't it? You always see what you want in the mirror. Be honest with yourself; you've been trying to get my attention all day and you finally have it. I can give you anything you want but that version of me isn't going to give you any of it. He values you like you wouldn't believe, but you've never been a love interest to him. He doesn't see you that way, but I do."

Feeling stone cold, Casey stood up and her reflection did the same.

"Acacia, you don't have to worry about that reality. There's no feeling guilty; we have our own reality right here if you choose it. This is the reality that reflects what you want, so come back over here and leave that One alone."

The One Casey knew didn't threaten or tell her what choice to make. Even when he'd been hunting her, he'd never ordered her to stay close. It was like he hadn't really wanted to turn her in. The warning tone this One had adopted set Casey on edge. "That's *my* One..." Casey stood face-to-face with her reflection.

"Acacia, that One isn't going to love you the way you want him to. He might not even live."

"That's okay," Casey said breathlessly, stepping back through the mirror and rushing back toward the real One.

The mirror disappeared as soon as Casey looked back at it and she felt a slight twinge of heartache, knowing what she'd left behind. It wasn't hard though to put that out of her mind with her One lying still on the floor. Casey knelt over him again, flipping him onto his back. His pale skin was nearly gray and his breathing barely echoed past his lips, eyes shut, the image of death.

From her pocket, Casey took one of the vials of demon blood she'd taken from the shapeshifting trader, relieved they were all still intact. She shifted and propped One's head against her leg before pulling the stopper out of a vial. The demon blood smelled awful, like rot and death, and Casey didn't want to think about what it might taste like. Regardless, she held

One's mouth open and let a single drop of the putrid black liquid drip onto his tongue, praying it would work. Casey had given up a more pleasant option for this and she needed *her* One back.

XIX

ONE

From the instant One felt the familiar unpleasant burning of demon blood in his mouth, he knew what Acacia had done. His most primal of instincts awoke first, coming out of brief dormancy at the taste of the toxin giving him new life.

Casey's face filled his vision when he blinked his eyes open. Her dark hair fell in strands around her face, loose from the ponytail she'd started the day with. She barely dared to breathe, eyes wide and hopeful. One caught a flash of movement as she replaced the vials of demon blood in her pocket, assuming One wouldn't notice. Even if One hadn't seen, he knew from the churning in his stomach and burning in his veins as his body ached for more.

Paramortals were never supposed to become mortal again. Demon blood was the poison keeping him alive. After so long without it, One was still closer to the edge than he could allow and his hands itched to snatch the vials away immediately with strength he didn't have yet.

"Did I do it right?" Acacia whispered.

One nodded and coughed, struggling to sit up, grateful for Acacia's hands on his shoulders, steadying him with a bright smile he didn't deserve from her. After everything that had happened, there was no reason she should be pleased to see him at all, much less beaming and clinging to his arm like One was some sort of resurrected hero. One narrowed his eyes and moved away from the touch.

Acacia pulled back as well, still smiling as she darted a hand out again to brush white hair away from One's face. "Are you alright?"

"We made it here intact so yeah, I guess."

"What is this place?" Acacia's eyes roamed the space, messy even by the usual standards with gold trinkets and ancient scrolls of parchment and stone tools on the countertops. The unusual decor had become normal for One, but it resembled a museum colliding with a suburban home to create the mess of relics everywhere. Acacia's eyes found One again, holding onto a bit of fear. "Are we safe here? Or are the rooms going to start moving again?"

One took a cautious deep breath, lungs protesting against living. "The house should be fine. You're safe. I'm surprised it held up as long as it did. I should've died. Everything around here should've fallen apart or stopped existing."

"Even Ezra?"

One's eyes shot up to connect with Acacia's. "Ezra found

you?"

"He's in his bedroom. The entire house turned into a maze and I was trying to find you and I found him first. He's fine, scared but fine. He's your brother? I didn't know you had a brother."

"There's a lot of things you don't know about me." One started to stand up, using the table for stability. Acacia kept close, helping him without being asked. One leaned against the wall for support, shuffling toward the stairs. "I'm going to go talk to him. You can wait here if you want."

"I can go tell him you're alright," Acacia followed, hands hovering nearby, "and you can stay here and rest. I'll get him to come down here or you can go see him after you sleep or something."

One hesitated on the top step. Before him was a small landing with a few closed doors and a hallway to one side. Light streamed from inside the two bedrooms and One turned toward the left door. "You're right. I don't want him to see me like this either. Help me into my room?" He pushed the door open weakly, letting Acacia follow him in. She looked around the space curiously and One felt briefly annoyed at himself at leaving a mess. Acacia walked to the middle of the room, unsure of where to place herself, then looked back when One didn't follow her.

"Acacia." Mustering all the strength he could find, One shot across the room, instantly holding Acacia with the tip of the crucifix nail against her throat, feeling her shoulders stiffen. He willed any weakness out of his gaze as he watched her, daring her to make a move. "Don't scream or try to run because there's nowhere to go. I'll let you out in a little bit but for now, don't test me."

"Wait—" Acacia blurted, keeping very still. "I have something you need."

"I'm well aware." One slid his other hand into her pocket, the glass vials of demon blood clinking together as One withdrew his prize. "I have to do what needs to be done. I'm sorry. Stay here and don't make any noise." With that, he let the point of the nail fall away and he escaped into the hall, shutting and locking the door from the outside.

A sigh escaped One's chest and he leaned against the wall, exhausted. His hand shook as he wrestled with the top of a vial, finally prying it off and hastily downing a drop. He bit back a scream, almost grateful for his lack of full awareness. Demon blood on its own was nobody's favorite. One knew he needed to eat something else and sleep too or his human side would surely end up sick, but time was still limited to turn Acacia in.

The demon blood settled at last and One stood up straight, rolling his shoulders and regaining a steady breathing rate before knocking quietly on the other upstairs bedroom door. Feeling a relieved smile flicker across his face, One knelt to hug Ezra as the little boy barreled toward him, rambling about what had happened to the house and about meeting Acacia.

One hovered a hand on Ezra's shoulder, knowing they couldn't actually touch. "I told you not to talk to anyone who came in here."

Ezra deflated, shrinking away. "But you like her. You said when you were home before. You let her come here."

Shaking his head, One stood up. "Acacia is not a friend, Ezra. She has to stay here for a while, but I'll deal with her soon and it'll go back to how things were for us. But the house is safe now for you to come out as long as you stay out of the basement and don't try to talk to Acacia. Okay?"

Ezra nodded. He brushed brown hair out of his eyes and hugged One again. "I'm glad you're back. I was scared."

"It's okay. I'm not going to let something like that happen again. I love you."

"Love you too."

One left the room with Ezra's bright eyes still watching him longingly. One shook his head slowly once the door was shut. He knew Ezra was going to be disappointed when this was over, and there was little way to avoid that. For now, he needed to go through with the plan, find a way to give Acacia to Gogmuth and get paid. One hoped he could trust Ezra not to talk to Acacia or try intervening when he returned to the basement to summon Gogmuth back. Any mistakes there could be catastrophic for all of them.

Feeling weak in the knees, One rested a hand on the wall, breathing deeply. He probably wouldn't have much luck forming a link with a demon at all if he tried anyway, still so low on blood. When he regained his strength, the unnatural pangs of remorse and compassion would fade too and he wouldn't have to pause and think about if turning Acacia in was really what he wanted to do. His veins flooded with demon blood again, he would just act, seeking the next dose, another day to survive.

"One?" Acacia's voice shook, muffled behind the bedroom door as she knocked. "I know you're out there. Let's talk about this, okay? We can agree on something, I'm sure. I'm not going to try to run if you open the door; I want to help you."

Resting his forehead on the door, One gritted his teeth. He wasn't surprised that the girl would protest her captivity, of course, but it didn't help the lonelier side of One that desperately wanted to let her out, wanted to reach an agreement.

"I can't." His voice cracked. "I can't save you or Ezra or myself or anyone. It's too late."

"That's okay," Acacia's voice was gentle. "You don't have to save everyone. Let me save you. Tell me how or... we'll figure something out."

"You *can't*," One repeated. "There's no saving me. And you're as good as dead too. You can't fight demons by being brave or whatever. You need the right kind of tools and even then, it wouldn't work."

"Can't you cast out demons? I don't know the Bible that well, but it's happened before, right? We can make them leave you alone.[15]"

"It doesn't work like that." One's hand reached out for the doorknob, but he pulled it back quickly, leaning against the wood instead. Breathing hard, he tried to release the catch in his mind begging to let Acacia be an ally instead of an enemy. "I already sold my soul a long time ago. That's why I need you, to turn you in so I can live and Ezra can live. Survival of the fittest, that's how this works. I captured you and I'm going to survive."

"So why haven't you turned me in then, One? I know you know how to do it. What happened back in that warehouse? I still don't understand."

"They were ready for us. Demon trade houses are kept off the grid so they can't be found but somehow heaven knew a deal was going down there today and they stepped in. The explosion was an angel trap, set to kill me and the other trader. It's a complication, but I'll find my way around it."

"How did the angels know we were going to be there?"

One's chest tightened in anger. "I don't know. Someone would've had to call them."

Acacia was silent as One's heart pounded loudly. "I think it was me. I've been praying all day because I thought you were an angel and I wanted to be saved and I asked for rescue. Do you think that could've been a part of it?"

Legs shaking, One slid down the wall to sit on the floor, burying his head in his clammy hands. Of course. That was a basic move of soul trading. It was the reason most soul traders didn't tell their victims about the celestial realm or the existence of paramortals. By proving the existence of demons to Acacia, One had proved the existence of angels as well.[16] Instead of destroying her, he'd rebirthed her faith.

That would prove to complicate Acacia's sale to a demon. Whether or not Gogmuth was even alive, One wouldn't be able to sell Acacia to any demon looking to commit her soul to the prison of eternal hell after death because she had the faith to fight it.[17] She'd summoned angels on her own; she was powerful like this, more powerful than One could contend with if she ever found out the weapon she held against him. One would have to sell her for slightly less than the original bounty because the most any demon could do with her was kill her and send her soul skyward.

Still, the price for that was better than dying in a few more days when this limited supply of demon blood ran out. Acacia had signed the contract on her own death but had gotten herself out of the worse fates that followed victims of soul trade. One needed to move fast and sell her before she got stronger. He rose up on his knees, lurching toward the staircase when another sudden wave of nausea weakened him and he collapsed again, groaning.

"One?" Acacia rose her voice, knocking on the door again.

She sounded much more worried than she should've for the life of a paramortal. "Are you okay?"

Instead of answering, One dug into his pocket and withdrew a vial of demon blood. He wouldn't be able to make an effective summons to a demon if he was still this weak. The drop of acrid liquid touched his tongue and One held back a yell, sitting against the bedroom door again, feeling Acacia's knocks on the other side like a headache, throbbing through his skull.

This weakness needed to be purged, decimated. There could be no trace of sympathy for the girl and no lingering suggestion to let her go. She could return to a normal life if One let her. In a day or two, she wouldn't remember any of this and she could live out her life as a good Christian girl and One would have to find another job or starve on the last doses of demon blood he held. The latter was much more likely so he knew he couldn't consider that an option. Acacia needed to die so One could live on a little longer.

"One?" Acacia asked again, voice barely above a whisper.

"Yes," One whispered back as the demon blood settled, "It was your doing. You brought the angels.[18]"

"I fought demons," Acacia breathed, sounding incredulous. "One, I fought demons and I'll do it again if it'll help you. I'll fight and I'll win!"

"You can't win against demons. The best you can do is survive them. That's what I do. I won't be able to escape hell forever, but I'm putting it off as long as I live and for that to work, I need to turn you in and get my reward."

"Then do that. Sell me, get paid, then I'll escape on my own. You don't need to always be the one saving me. I'm going to save you in return this time because I can fight demons. All I have to do is pray really hard, right?"

The demon blood lit a fire inside One and he exhaled, finally starting to feel normal again. "You're so stupid, Acacia." One stood up, paced the second-floor landing, and listened to the silence on the other side of the door. "You think it's that easy to escape a demon? You've never even seen one. I can promise that when you do, you'll be too scared to move, much less escape. You can't just *pray* and expect it to go the way you want."

Acacia's voice was close like she was sitting right on the other side of the door. "So what does it take? People fight demons, I know they do. If hell has its warriors, people like you, then heaven has to have its own fighters as well. How do I fight demons?"

"You can't. Not like this. People do fight demons, but it takes a lot of work. You haven't even been to church regularly in years so I don't know what you expect to be able to do."

"Tell me what you know. I'll figure it out from there."

One's eyes drifted closed. She would die trying. She would die anyway. One couldn't tell her answers that might get in the way of delivering her. He might as well though. One punched the wall hard enough to scratch his knuckles. The arguing back and forth in his brain was getting out of hand. He figured insanity must feel something like this. Was it too soon for another dose of demon blood? He needed to get back to full strength as quickly as possible without risking harm to himself. "Acacia, what do you know about how to get into heaven?"

Confusion edged Acacia's tone. "You have to believe that Jesus died for your sins[19] or something."

"Close. He died to take away the punishment that goes along with sin — death.[20] The important thing is that you have to believe it. God wants you, but you and everyone else on Earth can choose to reject this belief.[21] What do you know about the Holy Spirit?" The shakiness in One's hands was back. He wasn't strong enough yet and this wasn't helping. The last thing he should be doing was teaching scripture lessons so his prey could escape. It felt wrong. It was the opposite of everything he'd been programmed to do since the day he'd turned.

"The Holy Spirit is... like God but not?"

"The Spirit is part of God, specifically the part that is present for people on Earth. It lives in everyone, but only if they invite it in. You have to choose it. Do you see what I'm getting at here?[22]"

"Yeah, I have to choose God. So how do I do that?"

"You already have. If you have faith, that's the Holy Spirit at work. Demons work the same way though. They can't oppress you or harm you unless you let them. They can't fire until you give them the ammo. That's how you fight them." Pain opened up in One's chest again and he took another dose of demon blood to drown it out. He bit his bottom lip to keep back a cry of pain, feeling a bit of blood run down his chin from the bite marks. He gasped for breath and cursed. Why was he still trying to help Acacia? He'd already done too much by being kind to her on the journey downtown. There was no outcome that placed One on top aside from the outcome that ended with Acacia's death. One was betraying the entirety of hell by helping her, and it felt like someone taking a knife to his skull and splitting his brain in half.

"I don't get it," Acacia cried, pounding on the door again. "I don't understand how you fight demons like that."

"You don't," One growled, standing to his feet again. His vision tilted dangerously, but he stumbled toward the stairs. "You don't *fight* demons. You sit in that room and be quiet while I arrange to sell you." The war in One's mind raged on. It was too much trouble. Finding a buyer now would be hard. He was going to expend more demon blood trying to sell her than it was worth. He had supply now to last at least a few more days and he could find a relic hunting job again if he looked hard enough. This assignment wasn't worth it. He should just let Acacia go.

The demon blood spoke up from its raging path through One's veins. He needed this. There was only one way to stay alive and it was to take every opportunity to get more demon blood. Letting go of Acacia was a waste he couldn't afford and giving her over to hell's demons was another win for the home team that would strengthen their cause.

Acacia's voice followed him, strong and defiant. "What are you going to do if I don't cooperate? You can't kill me or I'm worthless to you."

The match struck and One whirled around to face the door again. He took another drop of demon blood and fingered the crucifix nail. "You're right; I can't kill you. But I can hurt you in ways you'll never recover from even if you do survive this." He drove the point of the nail straight through the wood of the door, relishing the sound of Acacia's high pitched scream as the wood splintered and the tip made itself visible to her. She was smart to fear it and painfully stupid to refuse to see One as a threat holding it. Without another word, One walked away and slunk down two flights of stairs to the basement.

By the time he reached the cement floor of the unfinished room, he had started chanting a familiar incantation and the pentagram taking up most of the floor space was glowing with the connection One had formed with the demon realm. One set the crucifix nail on the ground, just outside the circle before stepping inside the whirlwind of warm air and flying sand. The link let the weather in, filling the entire house with heat a mortal wouldn't be able to survive in for long. But One wasn't mortal and he had been living with this for decades. This was normal now and Earth had become frigid cold. After so much time spent trapped in the real world, the excruciating heat was welcome like a summer day after a long winter. One shed the scarf and fleece vest, tossing the extra clothing outside the link, then pushed up his sleeves and finished the incantation.

The sand that Gogmuth brought with him swirled the air and nearly brought One to his knees, but there was no sign of the demon's sneering face. The filth flew halfheartedly around the space, free from mastery.

"Gogmuth?" One feared the worst as he called out. When the heavens had learned of the trade going on, Gogmuth had likely been banished to the abyss, never to be heard from again. And that meant that One had brought in a bounty for nothing, that Acacia could not be delivered to the awaiting client she was promised to. Never again, One promised himself, would he take a soul trade job. It was always too messy, too risky, too uncertain. Minor demons seeking relics like One was used to collecting never fell under angel attack, only those dealing with the souls of mortals.

Severing the link, One swayed in place in the glowing circle on the floor, coughing up some stray sand, though much less than after his last encounter with Gogmuth. Sweat dripped from the ends of his hair and ran down his neck. Summoning was hard work at partial strength and the fires of the demon realm burned hot today, a sign that the Holy War outside was probably still battling on.

One brushed some of the dust off his shirt before giving up and removing it, tossing it over a chest of candles, perfumes, and metallic tools, all used for summoning. He dropped another dose of demon blood into his mouth, cringing at the burn, but relishing the feeling of power that came with renewing his former strength.

Muttering a new incantation, the pentagram glowed to life again, pulling One within to the same place where the job board was located. In the same way that paramortals could look for new job assignments, he could pawn off anything in his possession, treasures or souls. One had several items listed already, the torn curtain still wasting space somewhere upstairs among other things, heavenly trinkets that littered the floors and furniture of his house. Offers for relics were few and far between, not a reliable source of blood at all, but offers for souls usually brought quick results. Cowardly demons thrived here, not willing to place a bounty on a soul and risk being intercepted and destroyed like Gogmuth had. Some paramortals made their career out of capturing souls at random and hoping they weren't strong enough to fight back, selling them quickly for much lower prices than an assigned victim, but enough to live on.

Putting up the new listing took little time and One backed out of the pentagram when he'd finished and severed the connection. Hopefully, it wouldn't be long before a demon would answer him, looking for easy prey, already caught and mortally terrified: just the way demons liked their meals.

Tipping his head back again, One let two drops of demon blood slide down his throat and almost gagged. It was too much at once, but it felt great. The power that it brought was familiar and safe. He would get through this and never let his stock of demon blood get this low again, whatever it took. The realm would never flicker and start crumbling again and Ezra would never have to feel unsafe here. He would never have to wonder if something was wrong and they could go back to being a family again.

X X

CASEY

Casey knocked on the door and yelled for several minutes after One stopped responding, tears sliding down her face. The wood of the door was torn and splintered inward in a neat hole where One had stabbed through it with the nail. The hole was slightly off-centered and halfway up from the floor. If Casey had still been sitting against the door instead of moving to stand a few inches away, she very well could've been stabbed. Still, she had a feeling One hadn't been trying to hurt her, only scare her. It was infuriating, still feeling connected to him somehow, wanting so hard to see the good in him despite all the contrasting actions he displayed. He had to have a little good in him, Casey figured, or he would've found a way to get rid of her by now, if he really was trying to lose her.[23]

Only minutes later, Casey heard the lock click quietly open and Ezra poked his head in, green eyes wide. He looked over his shoulder before slipping inside and shutting the door again. Ezra ran forward, jumping into Casey's arms like she was familiar company instead of a near stranger. "I'm sorry, Acacia!" he whispered, pulling away to look her in the eyes. His own were saturated with ill-concealed fear. "I don't know what's going on. One said not to talk to you or let you out but I'm scared. He's not usually like this... and I'm sorry he yelled at you and locked you in here. I don't know... it seemed like he was fine before. The night before last night we sat out in the backyard for a while and watched the stars and he told me that I was the most important thing in the world to him and hugged me a lot and I asked if he was okay because he's not always like that but he said he was fine and I shouldn't worry. But I am worried."

Tears threatened Casey's eyes again. Ezra didn't even know all she did. Yesterday, she hadn't known who One was, what paramortals were, if demons really existed. Everything that had happened since meeting the white-haired half-demon had taken place in the span of only a day.

The bedroom had a window but the setting sun had finished its descent, leaving the room dim aside from a lamp on a bedside table which had been on since Casey had gotten there. The night before last, One had been looking for a job, desperately and dangerously low on demon blood, the drug keeping him alive. Of course, he would remind Ezra how important he was to him. Of course, he would act like nothing was wrong. Of course, Ezra would end up worried anyway.

Holding her arms out, Casey waited for Ezra to hug her, still hesitant after the last time her own hand had passed through his skin like he wasn't really there, but Ezra leaned against her with little difficulty. "It's okay. You're not going to get in trouble for talking to me. And don't be mad at One for yelling. It's just the way he is, right?[24]"

Ezra looked crestfallen, leaning his head on Casey's shoulder and allowing his hair to be stroked. "He wasn't always like that. I don't know when, but it was a long time ago and something happened and he changed. He was a lot nicer. He... didn't always go by the name One but I *can't* remember what his name was before but I feel like I should remember. And I remember him being different and he had a lot of friends and I had a lot of friends too who came over to play. Then something happened and it's been different. One is gone sometimes for a couple days and I can never leave and he spends a lot of time in the basement but he won't let me go down there. And... He's not happy anymore. Are you going to help him?"

Doing her best to organize all the new information, Casey patted the little boy's shoulder, still not as solid as he looked. "I'll do my best. I don't know what to do, but I'll figure it out. I really care about One and I want to do what I can for him and for you." Casey doubted Ezra knew about the separate realm from earth considering all the secrets One apparently kept from him, so she didn't ask about the chances of escaping. "Ezra, how long have you been here with One? You said it was a long time ago, so how old were you when things changed?"

Biting his lip, tears sprung into Ezra's eyes. "This age. And One was the same age too. But it's been so long. Every day happens the same and I think time has to be passing, but I don't feel any different now."

Casey figured magic was behind the lack of aging. If Ezra thought a long time had passed that he couldn't remember what One used to be like, it had probably been at least a few years. Casey couldn't imagine living Ezra's life, trapped in here, unsure of what was happening to his brother. But out of all the despairing information, Casey found a bit of hope. One hadn't always been like this. If he had changed once, he could change again. Even if it meant having to use her newfound abilities to fight demons, Casey would help One change again. She let go of Ezra and moved back to the door, ready to confront One.

Ezra followed close behind as Casey made her way downstairs. When Casey put her hand on the basement door, the little boy hesitated. There was no lock on the door so Casey figured the only thing that kept him out was One's order to stay away from the basement. Ezra obeyed One without question, unlike any kid Casey had met before, always on the prowl to disobey authorities.

Casey opened the door and was met with a wave of steaming warm air choking her. The entire house was hot, but it was worse down here. She looked down the staircase and locked eyes with One, looking back at her from the cement floor. He was shirtless and his eyes reflected the same burning rage as when he'd left. As much as Casey still wanted to love him, he looked scary.

Scowling, One took a step back and grabbed a wad of black fabric, pulling a short-sleeve t-shirt on, but not before Casey caught sight of an intricate black tattoo on his lower back.

Casey took a defiant step down the stairs, despite the unwelcome aura that made her feel as uncomfortable as the heat did. "One? What are you doing down here? It's a million degrees!"

No response met her other than a steady glare and Casey made her way slowly down the steps, feeling sweat run down her back. "Let me help you, One. We can find a way out of this if we work together. I never meant to make you angry. When I stole that demon blood from the trader, I was going to use it to help you. You didn't have to steal it from me. Trust me, I want you to be okay. Are you okay?"

"It doesn't matter," One shot back, taking a step toward the staircase. "You won't be my problem to deal with soon. All you've done is mess things up for me and I'll be happy when I can get rid of you."

The biting words stabbed at Casey's heart and she paused at the bottom of the staircase, feeling light-headed from the heat. "What did I do? I wasn't trying to make things hard for you; I didn't even know what was happening! Weren't you already low on demon blood? That's why you took this assignment. I got you more because I'm trying to help. Let me do something for you if I can. I care about you, One."

"Shut up." He turned away.

Casey shook her head and looked around the dim basement. Bare electric bulbs fought a losing battle against the shadows. Clutter lined the walls along with dust and even a few scorch marks. In the center of the room was a pentagram, much like the design on the floor of the trade house but smaller. It glowed like it had been used recently. Casey cocked an eyebrow. "One, you're summoning demons? Isn't it dangerous with everything that happened outside?"

"It's not dangerous. Shut up." One stood to the side, letting Casey get a good look around the space. "Just because that deal went bad doesn't mean others will. Someone out there will give me at least something for you, I'm sure."

A flicker of anger pulled Casey's frown down. This was not the One she knew; it was like she had stepped into another mirror dimension, but she knew this One was probably closer to who he usually was when he wasn't pretending to be nice to her. "You're going to sell me like cheap junk? That's still all I am to you?"

"Yes, and that's how it's supposed to be! I'm paramortal. You're human. You are nothing to me but a means of currency."

"I trusted you," Casey held One's gaze as long as she could before he looked away. "You're better than this. You showed me that you're better than this and you can do it again."

"You're wrong," One spat. "You trusted me because you're too stupid to question whether the stranger you followed was an angel or a demon. I never thought I was that subtle, but you still can't get it through your head that you are nothing to me but an expendable means to stay alive."

Casey's heart pounded with grief and she felt like crying. This wasn't her One. She knew it was the demon blood making him this way. She tried not to let her emotions show, setting her jaw firmly instead. "I'll run away. You said it's not safe to go back to earth but I'll take that risk. It's better than being stuck here with you."

One growled and lunged out, grabbing Casey's arm and yanking her away from the stairs. As she stumbled away, One froze and loosened his grip.

Still three steps up from the bottom, Ezra stood just as still as he had been through the entire conversation, eyes filled with tears and unfathomable pain.

Turning on Casey, One grabbed her again, throwing her to the floor. "You led him down here? This basement is dangerous! It's no place for a kid!"

Ezra's lips whispered wordless syllables until he got his bearings back enough to cry. "I knew something changed, One. You're different, really different. You said just because you don't look like you used to and mom and dad aren't here and my friends are gone didn't mean everything had to change.

You said you were always going to be the same and love me!"

"I do love you, Ezra." The ice in One's blue eyes melted immediately as he took a step toward the staircase. He knelt down and held his arms out. "Come on, let's get out of here."

Casey stood up slowly from the floor, aching. Her attention was more drawn to the touching scene in front of her as One led his brother back up the stairs. The sudden mood shift revealed to Casey just how capable One was of love. He wasn't violent, cold, and heartless like he acted. But Casey wasn't sure how to reach the deeper parts of him.

At the top of the stairs, One shot a look over his shoulder at Casey. "Stay down here. I'll deal with you in a minute."

"No!" Ezra pulled away from One and ran behind Casey. "Don't do anything to her, One! I like her and you like her, I know you do, even if you said all those bad things!"

Voice calm, One took the first step up to the second floor. "I know. I'm trying to talk things out with you if you'll let me. Let's go up to your room and talk, just the two of us."

Reluctantly, Ezra followed and Casey took a step back. The front door loomed in the corner of her eye, the means of escape from this realm. Casey couldn't imagine One leaving her alone on the ground floor with such an obvious exit, but it was starting to look like the best option. Of course, One had also said that there was a Holy War battle going on in the real world, but Casey took another step toward the entryway. She didn't want to hear anything else One had to say to her. She wanted to get out of here.

Casey pulled the door open, ignoring the sound of One shouting her name from behind her.

Before she even stepped all the way through the doorway, Casey found herself standing in the exact same spot she'd vanished from when the building had begun shaking.

The shaking hadn't stopped, Casey discovered when she opened her eyes, but instead had gotten much worse. The warehouse was devastated, the floor torn apart and the walls in pieces. Fragments of the ceiling lay in chunks on the ground. All around Casey was deafening noise and slaughter. Amidst the smell of electricity in the air and the settling dust and smoke, Casey thought she saw a flash of a giant creature, several times her height. Through the smoke, it appeared as little more than a shadow, a black shape with blurry edges. An inhuman scream exploded from its mouth as a glowing blade cleaved through its shoulder. A man-shaped silhouette of light cut through the smog like the sun shining through cloud cover and Casey rushed to cover her eyes, feeling it burn. The massive, hideous creature crashed to the ground only feet from where Casey stood and she shrieked, unheard over the boom of the impact she felt in the pit of her stomach.

The beast wasn't dead yet, Casey saw and heard by the fierce roar as it struggled to get back up. The man of light fought back, a metallic clang ringing through the destroyed warehouse, full of similar tussles, as their weapons met. A shower of sparks flew off the connected swords and Casey fell backward as red-hot sparks littered the ground near her. She screamed again, invisible to the war around her as the beast was knocked back as well. Casey's mind filled with images of being crushed like a pebble beneath the creature and she tried her best to run away.

From behind her, a low growl made the hairs on the back of her neck stand up and she turned. Another shadow beast materialized out of the smoke cover in front of her. This one was smaller but scared Casey even more, watching it move toward her, red eyes blinking out of a dark mist. The next growl poured from where the shadow's mouth would be, sounding pleased.

Casey couldn't move, kneeling on the ground, helpless.

"Stay back, hellspawn!"

Casey looked behind her to see One only inches away, the crucifix nail in hand and an unshakable challenge in his eye.

One took a step closer to Casey, not taking his eyes off the demon. "You can't have her. She's protected by bounty laws."

The demon snarled again, voice muffled like it was being heard through a pane of glass. "You're the mortal who started this. Not dead yet. Lucky Gogmuth's dead. Lucky me."

"She's not for sale," One said, resting a hand on Casey's shoulder and vanishing from the battlegrounds again.

Back in the foyer of the house, it was as if nothing had happened outside at all. The war was gone, the smoke was gone, the feeling in the air like a building thunderstorm, gone. Ezra watched from the top of the staircase as Casey blinked with shock and ran her fingers over the hardwood floor, so peaceful and ordinary in comparison with the broken concrete of the warehouse. Casey cried, tears of fear and horror and relief, all at once.

One sighed from above her and took a step inside. "Get up. You're okay."

"I'm sorry," Casey choked. "One, I'm sorry, I didn't mean to."

The blank expression on One's face didn't change but he offered a hand down.

Casey reached up and pulled herself to her feet, following One as he let go again and started for the stairs. He mumbled something to Ezra who escaped behind his bedroom door. Casey almost wished the little boy would stick close; One was so much milder with Ezra around, not as prone to yelling or lashing out.

Instead, One led Casey into his own bedroom where he had locked her before. This time, the door closed with a soft click behind both of them and One rubbed his eyes as he leaned against the wall. His face was taut and he looked paler than usual. Worry for One never left Casey's mind but it was stronger now. "What's wrong?"

One shook his head, exhaling shallowly. "Demons suck. If they want something from you, chances are they're going to try taking over your body and taking what they need for free rather than playing by the rules."

Eyes widening, Casey tried to read into One's expression. "Like possession? Have you been possessed by a demon before?"

"It's never happened to me before, but it's not something you want to happen under any circumstance." One turned and lifted the back of his t-shirt, revealing an intricate black tattoo, the one Casey had glimpsed in the basement. Lines marked the skin around it, turning it red and irritated as if it had been scratched by something with four large claws. "Anti-possession rune," One explained. "It keeps the demons out but it burns like hell when they try." Taking a few deep breaths, One crossed the room and sat down on a blue beanbag.

In the panic of being locked in before, Casey hadn't bothered to study the room, but it wasn't what she had been expecting. From someone like One, Casey expected the room to be bare and minimalistic with only the necessities and just as cold an atmosphere as he seemed to give off. For some reason, Casey expected a bedroom that looked more like a prison cell, thin blanket, and bars over the window. Casey couldn't imagine ever needing a blanket in a house as warm as it was here, but there was indeed a blanket on the large bed. When Casey ran her fingers over the coverings, they were soft and plush, maybe softer than hers at home. The walls were light blue and glowed in moonlight drifting in through the window's sheer curtains. More gold trinkets littered the floor and a bookcase, crammed with junk that may or may not hold significance. Clothes, mostly gray, spilled out a laundry hamper and there was a pile of candy wrappers on one side of the bed, rumpled sheets pushed back and half- falling onto the floor.

"I didn't take you for an ordinary, slobby teenager." Casey almost smiled.

"I can't be comfortable in my own house?" One shifted in the beanbag, accentuating how comfortable he was. "I wasn't exactly expecting guests."

Casey let the smile take over her face and she perched on the foot of the bed. Really, this didn't feel so different from lounging in Rose's bedroom. She felt natural with One, relaxing across the room. Still, the peace of the moment didn't distract Casey from the reality of the present situation for long. She looked at her companion. "One... I'm sorry for running away. What happened out there?"

One sighed. "Congratulations, you're on the very short list of humans who have seen the Holy War in action and lived to tell the tale."

XXI

ONE

With Acacia's eyes watching him with hope, fear, and a little bit of admiration, One didn't have much choice but to tell the truth. He had never been able to lie to her that well.[25] "Celestials — angels and demons — can't take physical form, but sometimes the celestial realm and the terrestrial realm clash. You saw them as light and dark; that's not their true form, but it's as close as you'll see of an angel or demon on Earth. Very few humans have ever gotten to see that."

"What about paramortals? Have you seen angels and demons like that before?"

"Not like that... I doubt many of us have. But we see angels and demons in their true forms in celestial realms all the time. It's not something you want to see." One pushed hair away from his face, studying the far wall. "The Holy War has been getting more and more intense in the past few decades and stuff like this has been happening more and more often: angels intercepting demon trade, demons crawling up to the surface to try to fight an angel while the opportunity is there. That feeling in the air like static electricity? Celestials put off tangible energy just by existing. It tends to bleed through the borders of realms. The terrestrial realm and the celestial realm overlap enough that you can feel it or a demon could reach through and take you if you aren't protecting yourself. But battles like this rarely last very long so we should be able to get out of here at some point soon."

Acacia was frozen in place on the bed looking terrified and rightfully so. It was a pity she wouldn't remember any of this or she would have a great story to tell. Realistically, she wouldn't survive long enough to tell it anyway.

The girl's eyes wandered around the room as she processed. From the ground, she picked up a gold necklace with a blue sapphire pendant. "What is all this gold and stuff around your house?"

"Again, that's the most pressing question you have?" One almost let a smile touch the surface. "It's celestial treasure. I steal it. That's my job.[26]"

"Then why do you keep so much of it? I didn't take you for a hoarder."

One looked around the room. Usually, the treasures of gold, silver, brass, and bronze stayed piled on empty shelves and countertops but since the near-loss of One's life, most of it had tumbled onto the floor as the realm began to crumble. It was more evident this way how much treasure One really kept around, a hundred times more pure and valuable than any precious metal on Earth and yet, nearly worthless as currency for demon blood.

Acacia smirked and tossed the bed sheets so they lay a little neater. "I thought I was messy, but you keep everything, don't you."

"I'm not a hoarder. There aren't many things in this house that are real so I hang onto the things that are real like that treasure." Seeing the confused expression on Acacia's face, One elaborated. "That bed, that lamp, that book by your hand, none of it is real. This is a separate realm from Earth, but it's not a fully physical realm. If I took that book and walked through the front door, it wouldn't come with. The stuff I collect on jobs is real and it might be worth something at some point if I can find the right buyer."

Acacia still looked amused. "If I asked Ezra, would he agree that you're a hoarder?"

One narrowed his eyes, less amused. He would probably regret giving a straight answer. He didn't owe Acacia anything, much less the truth: the most valuable thing he had in his possession. "No. Ezra can't see any of it. He's part of this realm and he can't see anything I bring from celestial realms."

The teen girl watched One without blinking, deciding how to proceed. If she was smart, she wouldn't bring up the make-believe image of a child One kept in his house. "So where do you get the treasure? I can't imagine you find it along the way trying to kidnap people like me."

"I'm a relic hunter actually." One's usual title brought with it a swell of pride. "And I'm good at it. Demons get strength from stolen angelic items but it's hard for them to get into the angelic realm undetected so that's why they get paramortals like me to do it for them. Soul trading is the branch that steals human souls and commits them to an eternity in hell."

"But treasure isn't worth as much as souls, right?"

"No. Why does that matter?[27]"

"If you're so good, why can't you handle soul trade?"

Was Acacia trying to bite the hand that fed her? One almost considered kicking her back out into the midst of the Holy War and seeing what she had to say about that. "I don't like it." One said, emotionless. "It's not as fun and it's harder to stay off the radar. I have a bit of a reputation. Besides, soul trade is messy and you're more likely to end up dead than with any sort of reward. It pays better, but I don't usually need that. I just need enough demon blood to survive and I can get that relic hunting. I've worked soul trade before, but it isn't my strong suit. Things like this happen and now I still don't know what to do with you. I don't really want to hand you over, but demons are still looking for you and I don't know how far you'd make it anyway. I'd probably be killed for letting you go."

Having fallen quiet, Acacia played with the gold chain in her hands. "You don't have to pretend you don't want me turned in."

"I don't. I wish I knew how to get you out of this." One stared at his hands, crossed with faint white scars. The larger line under his eye itched at the memory of the last soul trade job he worked, almost a full decade ago. "Not that it means anything, but you can keep that necklace if you want. I don't need it for anything."

Acacia's eyebrows rose in surprise and she smiled, trying not to look at One directly as she clasped the chain around her neck. "It means a lot to me. Thank you." Her expression darkened again. "So what's really going to happen to me? Realistically. How does soul trade work? I know you were trying to sell me somehow when you were in the basement. But outside you said... I wasn't for sale."

"Sorry for sending mixed signals. I'm having a hard time with committing treason but I don't want to turn you in.[28] If it had worked the first time, before the angel trap, I probably wouldn't have done anything to stop it. What happens to a soul trade victim really depends on the demon. If you were lucky, Gogmuth — the demon that hired me to capture you — would've claimed your soul and sent you back home and you would live out your life, die, and go to hell. If you weren't as lucky, he might've just killed you and you would spend eternity in hell starting now. I'm guessing you call yourself a Christian but don't act on it, right? Until today, you didn't really stand behind your faith, did you. That makes you a prime target."

Nodding, Acacia fingered the necklace. "I didn't mean to..."

"It happens to people all the time when they lose their faith," One shrugged. "It seems like a big deal talking about it, but it happens to an astonishing number of people. One day they're sort of Christian, and the next, it's faded away and they don't think to call themselves a believer anymore. They don't remember but they were taken just the same as you were and their soul was claimed. If half the victims of soul trade knew what was happening to them, their faith probably would've been renewed like yours. I don't know if that'll make your case better or worse though." An itch nagged at the back of One's head. He wanted more demon blood. He was strong enough now to get by, but the urge didn't leave.

"You said if I was lucky I would've been released or killed. What happens if I'm an unlucky soul trade victim?"

One staunched the urge for demon blood. It brought out the worst in him. It made him angry and rude. The peaceful conversation with Acacia wouldn't last long and he wanted it to last a lot longer. He shifted deeper into the beanbag, hoping for comfort to quell his addiction. "If you're really unlucky, they make you into someone like me, paramortal. Most don't make it, killed in the process. But if you do, you spend the rest of eternity working for demons to get the next dose of demon blood until you die and end up in hell anyway. I would've died if you hadn't stolen that demon blood from the shapeshifter though I don't know how much longer I'll live unless I can find a good job to pay me enough to get by for a while. It's not a life

I'd wish on anyone; I was hoping you'd get lucky."

"If it's such a bad life, why don't you let yourself run out of demon blood?" Acacia's expression softened. "I wouldn't want you to die, but... you're not happy. I was right before, wasn't I. You are sick in a way and you're miserable because of it."

"It's not that easy, Acacia." One laid back and closed his eyes. As comfortable as he could pretend to be, he was sick. He had poison in his blood and the only cure was to lay down and let death take him. Only then would the suffering be over. And yet, that would be only the beginning. "They know exactly how to keep you here forever. They give you exactly what you want and as soon as you have it, you know it's not worth it, but it might be worth putting off death a while longer for it. People want to be unhurtable and they end up made of metal like the trader on the train. They want to be someone they're not and they start shapeshifting like the last trader. For me, my paramortality is keeping Ezra alive in this realm. If I don't think too hard, I can pretend he's real and we're still a family."

Without responding, Acacia stood up and sat down again on the beanbag next to One, touching his shoulder. "You can tell me. I already know how the story ends so I'm not going to judge you."

It had been years since One had cried, maybe decades. Immortality made very few things seem worth feeling emotional over. It had been twenty-five years since the accident, but it was still the clearest memory One possessed. "I was eighteen, Ezra was ten. We were home while our parents were out. I was in my room and Ezra fell down the stairs and died. I was listening to music and didn't hear so I didn't know anything had happened until mom and dad came home and found him. It... It wasn't my fault, but I should've been taking better care of him. Ezra and I were raised Christian and I'm sure his soul went to the right place, but I was so mad at God. That's what demons love, faith that dies, anger that springs up in its place. It makes you a great paramortal."

"The demons let you have Ezra back," Acacia summarized, brushing her fingers up One's arm. "So you became what they wanted you to be."

One stood up abruptly. It had been decades since anyone had touched him like that, without ulterior motive, pity, or thinly veiled disapproval. Acacia still loved him and it left a tingle up One's bare forearm. He stalked to the window, watching the black midnight stand still, refusing to cry in front of Acacia. "It's not worth it. No matter what they offer you, powers or security or future, it's better to die before they convert you because it's impossible to go back once you sell your soul. I could let my paramortality wear out and accept death, but it would mean Ezra died a second time on my watch and it wouldn't change the fact I wasn't there to catch him when he fell. I wish I would've died while I was still mortal, before they let me have him back. I can't let him go but I have to kill people like you who don't deserve it either. I'm not strong enough for this life. I need to die."

Silently, Acacia got to her feet and slid her arms around One's waist from behind, pushing her face against the back of his neck. As deplorable as One managed to be, Acacia was still following, still chasing, never giving up. She had to have a limit somewhere but One hadn't found it yet. He hoped he would never find the limit.[29]

One suppressed a shiver. "It's awful, what you go through to become paramortal. Your mortal body is destroyed and recreated. My parents are probably still out there somewhere but they wouldn't recognize me like this. I hate everything I am now, even though I am the reason for everything I became. But no one ever tries going back to who they were before because they're too busy with this now. They fill you up with demon blood and let you have the one thing you want more than anything else so you know what it feels like to be celestial, immortal, unstoppable. Then they take it all away and leave you empty. Demon blood is so addictive and some paramortals spend their lives trying to get as much as possible, wanting to get back to the feeling of infinite power but you can't ever get that back. It drives them insane. I got what I wanted when I got Ezra back, but I've been eighteen for twenty-five years and I'll be eighteen until I die, the day I'm brave enough to stop stealing relics from heaven and let Ezra die too."

Acacia shifted, pulling One into a real hug like on the train but this time, One buried his face in Acacia's shoulder, hiding tears. She slid fingers through his hair and whispered. "I love you for who you are now. You're not a bad person because of the mistakes you made. You can always be forgiven.[30]"

"I can't. That's part of the deal. Selling your soul isn't something easily undone or more people would escape this life. You can't just say sorry and go back to the way things were." Every paramortal One had ever met wished for death in some way, wished for the suffering of life to end, wished they didn't have to keep making the same mistakes over and over again. But there was no way out of the addiction with death as the only cure and hell the only rehab. No one survived this to give encouragement. Every paramortal was a half-dead cog in a machine grinding onward without regard for its inner workings.

One had thought for a moment that Acacia would understand with all her compassion and raw humanity. Somehow, One thought she might have an answer as the only person to ever love One again. Instead, she pulled away, leaving One feeling cold where she had been touching him. The bedroom door opened and footsteps pattered down the stairs. A familiar squeak of the front door signaled that Acacia had left for good. She would rather risk stepping back into the Holy War than stand so close to someone who had betrayed everything he'd ever loved to become something that heaven despised. One rested his head on the window. He couldn't blame her.

"God, please save me. I don't want to live like this anymore. Take me back, I'm sorry." But One figured only silence heard the prayers of a demon.[31]

Part 3

XXII

CASEY

Once the idea had planted itself in Casey's mind there was no shaking it. She couldn't place where the thought had come from so she knew it must have come from where all blessed inspiration came from.

Of course, One would veto the plan, say it was too dangerous, not worth trying to save his life, but Casey didn't want to hear that. There were angels right outside the door and if there was a good God in this universe, His angels would find a way to help One. He wasn't destined to spend his life as a slave of hell. He deserved so much more than that. Repentance should work for him if he was sincere and Casey was positive he was.

Of course, the thought of running back out into the midst of the Holy War terrified Casey, but if she missed this opportunity, she didn't know when she was ever going to find herself in the presence of an angel again to request help from the heavens.

Casey sprinted through the front door, stumbling back into the trade house. Turning in a full circle, she was shocked to find it changed from either of the first two times she'd entered it. With the battle raging around her before, Casey hadn't seen the extent of the damage to the warehouse, but the smoke and dust had cleared by now and she saw it all. The ceiling and roof were gone, the pieces pushed to the sides and corners of the space. The support columns that used to hold it up had been uprooted and tossed aside like twigs. Crevices and chasms had opened up in the floor, crisscrossing the full area like a melting icecap with fissures Casey could fall into. Scorch marks raced across every intact surface and a massive set of claw marks etched the nearest wall, turning solid brickwork into gravel on the floor.

Looking up, Casey found the night sky awaiting her, calm and dark as ever. Life around the trade house continued as normal and Casey could see cars cruising the streets. The demon magic surrounding the building must be insanely powerful that no one outside seemed to notice an entire downtown structure had been decimated.

The foolishness of the plan nagged at Casey and she was suddenly very glad the Holy War battle seemed to have waned. The glimpse she caught of the fight had scared her, but clearly not enough. Looking around at the destruction around her, Casey knew she wouldn't have made it more than a minute out here on her own, much like the last time.

Casey took a hesitant step on the cracked ground. She couldn't tell which side had won this battle. There were no bodies, blood, or broken weapons on the ground to give any indication that angels and demons had fought here or who had sustained damages to their army. The real outcomes of battle were probably more visible in the celestial realm where the battle had truly taken place.

Knowing as Casey did the carnage that had swept through the building, the eeriest part of it now was the silence left behind. Not a breath of wind flowed through the shattered husk of the building and the air felt warm, heavy and alive as if it were charged with electricity.

That feeling of energy had been present before and One had said something about it being caused by the presence of celestials. The battle must have ended recently if the static still remained.

Casey turned a full circle and surveyed the air around her. There was no trace of an entrance back into One's realm. She knew she would never understand the magic behind it but it baffled her to look for physics in it. There must not be any way inside except for with One. Gingerly stepping forward again, Casey traced a path of intact floor until it broke apart, the bottom crashing down into an endless chasm; Casey felt very small, wandering in the wake of the battle. In the center of the room, she could see the broken up image of the pentagram and she headed toward it for a closer look now that she wasn't being dragged inside, screaming and terrified.

The design was large and Casey had to take several steps from the edge to the middle where she turned to look at the room around her. She closed her eyes, wondering if she could feel some sort of presence if she concentrated, if she could pray hard enough to bring an angel back.

The hairs on the back of Casey's neck stood on end, freezing her where she stood. A faint rattling sound fluttered behind Casey and darkness nestled in her heart, sending fear shooting through her.

A few feet away was a large opening in the floor, black as if shadows had been poured into it. Some of the liquid shadow seemed to be creeping out of the crevice and spreading across the floor. It made a whispery hissing sound, like wind tossing leaves on dying trees.

Demons were down there, Casey knew. If there was an entrance to the alleged demon realm beneath the Earth's surface as One had alluded to, this had to be it. Nothing good could come from this place.

On the other hand, if demons were down there, maybe that could be the solution to freeing One from his slavery. All Casey had to do was make sure her faith was stronger than the demons and she knew she could make it happen if she focused. She'd never felt closer to God and she believed she was called into the demon realm to show off her new abilities and set her friend free.

"Acacia!"

One's shout from behind her made Casey blink and snap out of her stupor. She hadn't realized she was moving, but stood now on the edge of the crevice, looking down into the blackness. In the spot she'd first appeared from, Casey saw her companion, moving toward her quickly, navy eyes wide.

"Acacia, step away from that. What are you doing?"

"I'm going to save you." Casey smiled, looking down into the blackness. "I think the answer is down here somewhere. I'm going to find it."

"There are no answers down there, Acacia," One said firmly. "That's the demon realm you're talking about. Listen to yourself."

Oh, Casey was listening to herself. The whisper in her mind pushed her onward and she sat down on the edge of the chasm, feet dangling into the blackness. "I'm going to save you all by myself," she whispered, pushing off with her hands and dropping down into the abyss.

XXIII

ONE

Rational thought was the furthest thing from One's mind as he sprinted forward and threw himself into the chasm, scrambling down the sheer rock face, jumping between small cliffs to descend lower beneath the ground. With the descent came darkness and One did more stumbling than chasing. More alarming than the faint echoes of Acacia's screams was the unmistakable rattle of demon wings fluttering. They had probably been waiting for her just below the surface, tempting her beyond the magical border of the demon realm so they could grab her as soon as she crossed the threshold into the demon realm.

One barreled faster down the fractured rock face toward the awaiting nest of demons somewhere far below. He couldn't get too far behind or he would lose track of Acacia and probably never find her again. The demon realm was big and confusing and only demons knew the best hiding places.

Demons weren't supposed to steal a paramortal soul

trader's capture away from them, a rule established eons ago with the creation of soul trade. It was hard for demons to get their hands on humans since they couldn't take on a physical form in the terrestrial realm; they relied on paramortals to bring the souls of the weak and unbelieving. To ensure paramortals would still work for them, demons promised to buy and sell fairly. The demon who had stolen Acacia was a rule breaker, not uncommon among minor devils, but an even bigger problem for One to deal with. There was no way to keep Acacia safe from a wild card like that.

Running harder, One wondered if he was fast enough to catch up to the rogue demon and his capture. A list of promises skimmed through One's mind, promises of what he would do when he caught up. This demon surely didn't know that One held an immortal weapon and would be promptly gouging out the heart of the thief. It would be the last time the creature made assumptions about weak prey.

Shuddering with rage, One skidded on an unseen patch of loose rocks and fell to his knees. His jeans were already torn from being thrown by the angel trap and fresh blood spilled out.

He paused, breathing hard as his hands and knees bled over the stone. He didn't usually bleed this much. Demon blood usually staunched the flow quicker, but he probably wasn't as strong as he could be yet. Gingerly sitting down, One pulled a vial from his pocket, dropping a burning dose down his throat, eyes shut, muscles clenched, biting back a groan of pain as it took hold. He felt stronger again, but it didn't dig the gravel out of his skin.

One shook his head, annoyed he would be so reckless in such a dire time. He didn't think he usually acted like this, impulsive and impatient enough to go after a demon on foot. When had he lost the self-preservation that usually drove his actions?

The fact of the matter was he couldn't catch up with a demon on foot and he didn't need to. If he had stopped to think for a single instant before rushing after Acacia, he would've realized the better solutions. Demons and paramortals had agreed on a set of laws for this reason. Justice would be enforced in this issue to preserve the contract between the two entities.

One closed his eyes, opening them again to the inside of his home realm and the familiar front entryway. After confessing to Acacia the realm wasn't reality, it was harder to pretend it was, but One ignored it for the comfort home always brought. Standing at the top of the staircase, Ezra watched silently, not content to follow orders and stay in his room when he thought something big was happening. One smiled with a pang of guilt. He hadn't meant to run off again without explaining anything, always trying to be as open with Ezra as he could. He didn't take for granted the opportunity to have his little brother back.

With effort, One rose to his feet from the doormat. "Hey.

Sorry, I don't have a lot of time to talk right now, but I'll tell you everything when I get the chance. Alright, Ezra?"

Ezra didn't look convinced. "Where's Acacia?"

"I'm going to get her back," One promised, heading for the basement stairs. "Hang tight, buddy. We're all going to be okay."

"You're bleeding, One."

"I know." One hid his face in the doorway to the basement stairs. "I'm okay, I promise. Just let me take care of this and—"

"I don't want you to go down to the basement." The little boy leaned against the wall, looking at One with betrayal in his eyes. "It's scary down there. There's a bad man there who told me I'm not real."

One froze and looked up at his little brother. "Who's down there?"

"I don't know," Ezra shook his head, "but I saw him when you were outside. He said his name was Thastrok and I'm not real."

In a single exhale, One tried to expel the fear, anger, and desperation all building pressure inside his chest. It didn't work. Tears threatened his eyes for the second time that day and One turned away from the basement door to look at Ezra, sitting on the top step of the staircase he'd died on. One moved slowly up the stairs and rested a hand on the image of Ezra's shoulder, where he would be if he was real. One looked into his green eyes, the same color as their parents' had been. One's blue eyes had always been the anomaly, even then. Even before the color had seeped from his skin and hair, leaving Ezra a darker, richer reminder of what he used to look like too. "Did Thastrok scare you?"

Ezra nodded, a few tears sliding down his round cheeks.

"That's why I tell you not to go down there. If I'm not home, I can't protect you from the scary things in the basement. I promise when I'm done with this job, I'll tell you everything you want to know. I know you have questions I've never answered. Acacia's in danger and I need to save her so I don't have time right now, but I will tell you everything. I owe you the truth because I love you, Ezra."

"Am I real?" Ezra whispered, shoving his face into One's chest.

Threading his fingers through the boy's hair, One closed his eyes. If Ezra was real, he would feel the ever-present heat in the house from the gateway to hell downstairs. If Ezra was real, he would've aged in the last twenty-five years they'd been here together. If Ezra was real, he'd be able to step outside the house and enjoy Earth again. If Ezra was real, One would feel his tears soaking his t-shirt. One wished more than anything he could feel his brother's tears in his shirt. "Yes, you're real," One lied, pulling away. "I'll be back soon. Stay out of the basement. Thastrok can't scare you up here."

Wordless, Ezra watched One descend the stairs and disappear into the basement. The space was silent and empty, but the pentagram glowed softly like it had been used recently. To get in touch with Thastrok, Ezra would've had to step inside the pentagram and the mental image scared One more than he would like to admit. Demons liked keeping tabs on the paramortals they created. The powerful celestial had probably gotten plenty of amusement from watching Ezra squirm under the realization that his existence was a lie, a hologram created for One as Thastrok stripped him of his mortality. One had been beaten, broken, skinned, burned, torn limb from limb to create the part-demon he was now, all to preserve the memory of the green-eyed boy upstairs. And even that was falling apart now.

One stepped into the pentagram, feeling Thastrok's presence surrounding him, hearing the faint laughter that had filled the chamber so long ago while One had screamed, begged for death, begged to be damned to hell when that was the better option. One was tired of fighting, but he spoke the incantation, ready to fight again now for Acacia's life.

XXIV

CASEY

Hands found Casey when she slipped off the edge of the concrete floor into the chasm. Like a switch flipping, it didn't seem like a good idea anymore, but a quiet voice in her mind had made it sound brilliant just a second ago.[32]

She screamed. The skin of the hands was wrinkled and cold and calloused, wrapping around Casey. The hand must be huge, she knew, to hold her arms at her sides as the creature attached to it skittered further down into the darkness, too fast for Casey to get a good look at it. She screamed until all that tumbled out of her mouth were harsh whispered calls for help.

The heat rose quickly as she descended, the same kind of heat she'd felt in One's home realm and she knew without asking the question she was in the demon realm. The creatures down here weren't shadows, they were real. They could touch her and steal her away and kill her without lifting a finger.

The darkness gave way gradually to a brighter-lit tunnel cut into the solid rock and Casey looked around her with horror. The demon holding her had to be three times her height standing up, but just as fearsome crawling through the tunnel on all fours. Additional, mutated hands held her with shriveled, black fingers, complete with long, dirty claws. Casey was afraid to move, sure the claws were going to cut her if she struggled. This demon could eat her alive and the hunger that flashed in its red eyes told Casey it very well might.

As the demon ran with her in its grip, Casey started praying. It was the only thing she could think to do, the only thing that might make a difference. The demon stumbled and growled at her. It paused long enough to shake her in its fist. Casey cried out again. It hadn't been pleasant, but she thought maybe prayer may have actually worked against the demon somehow. If that was all it took, maybe she really could fight demons.

Before Casey had the chance to try again, the demon slowed its run, trotting out of the tunnel into an enormous cavern. In front of her lay a stone temple that looked straight out of a history textbook. Fires burned to light the giant space from every crevice in the temple and cast an orange glow on the rocky surfaces. Creatures — more demons, Casey knew — dashed between buildings and along walkways, carrying out tasks she couldn't hope to imagine.

Getting a good look at the demon that had taken her, Casey realized it was actually two. The larger stood up, a towering pale monstrosity, strong with powerful muscles and hard, black eyes. The smaller clung to the first's back, finally releasing Casey from its black claws and letting her stumble away on the hot, rocky ground. She was sure she was going to be sick, feeling the monster's claws still on her skin. Instead, she trembled silently, looking up at the large creatures. She had been so sure she could fight a demon through sheer willpower, but faced with physical adversaries so imposing, she lost the bravado she'd been holding onto.

"You don't scare me! I'll kill you!" Casey yelled, her voice cracking. One's description of being turned paramortal haunted her thoughts, reminding her of fates worse than death. She couldn't fight demons; she was lost, helpless, weak.

The larger demon bent over to look her in the eye, its serious expression unwavering. Dread filled her heart with a fire she couldn't control, her last defense against the fearsome creatures. "On your own, never." The massive beast's voice rumbled.

Scrambling toward her, the smaller demon had a manic smile on its twisted face. "She will try though! That is why you like her, because she will try what she knows will not work, won't she![33]"

"Get away from me!" Casey screamed. There wasn't anywhere to run. Behind her was the large temple and countless more demons and the two watching her wouldn't let her get far anyway. "You can't touch me! I'm a child of God and you have no power over me!"

Both demons faltered but came closer again. The bigger blinked down at her. "You have never known life without me. You may not recognize this form but I am Pride and I have never left you, from the moment of your first success."

Casey had never hated her own thoughts and feelings before, but she started to. She wouldn't know life without Pride, and that was undeniably true. She stomped her foot at the demon. "I don't care! I rebuke you! I'll fight you until you leave me alone!"

"A worthy battle," the demon mused. "I accept that challenge."

Casey stood her ground. There was no reason she couldn't master this demon. Sure, it had roots in her mind, but she was aware of it now and she wouldn't let it continue on as it had. She turned to look at the smaller of the two demons, creeping around beside her. "What are you supposed to be then?"

Chuckling, the demon darted forward and pushed Casey to the ground, standing over her and looking victorious. "You don't know me yet, but you'll soon know all about me so remember my name well." Breath warm and putrid, the demon leaned down to hiss in Casey's face. "Rebellion.[34]"

Gagging as Rebellion slobbered on her, Casey scooted away on her back across the stone floor. "I'm not a rebel though. I follow rules and I'm a good person. You don't have any power over me."

"You're not a rebel? That's cute." The demon scampered

behind Casey, sliding a clawed finger along the back of her neck. "You follow the rules, respect your family and your friends — oh, well, most of the time. We can forget about cheating on your boyfriend, right? It's an easy mistake to make and it's not like you did any harm while you were making kissy faces at your little halfling demon friend."

The finger left Casey's neck and something fell into her lap: the gold necklace One had offered to her. The blue pendant glittered in the dim firelight. "I didn't... cheat. I didn't even kiss One. It was an illusion and I chose the real world over that world. I care about Dylan and I would never do anything to hurt him. I don't want to act out and I'm not going to. I have a future and you can't take that away from me! I'm in charge here, not you!"

Pride almost smiled, reaching out and pushing Rebellion to the side, blocking its animalistic crawl toward Casey. "You heard her. She's in charge of her own life."

An uneasy feeling crawled into Casey's stomach, but she crossed her arms defiantly against the two demons. "Yeah. You can't make me do anything bad. Just let me go already. I won't put up with this anymore!"

"Let you go?" Pride cocked his head at her. "I thought you were going to take us down? Which is your intent?"

"U-um..." Casey glanced around her at the demon temple. "If I say let me go, what will you do?"

"Take you back home." Pride nodded like compliance was

standard. "This realm is not yours to inhabit."

Casey got to her feet, trying to look stronger than she felt. "Take me back home then. I need to... I'll figure out how to fight you once and for all and I'm going to save myself and One so he doesn't have to fear you either."

"We'll be awaiting your attack then," Pride said. "I wish you the best of luck."

Casey took a hesitant step toward the tunnel they'd come through. Neither of the demons made any move to stop her. She passed by Rebellion, feeling hot breath in her face, but still no action against her. Casey stepped out of the cavern, back into the smaller tunnel, many feet taller than she was. She closed her eyes and took a deep breath. Lingering fear shook her and she let it, now out of range of the demons. Their threats clung to her and she almost didn't want to go home. She wanted to stay and fight, she wanted to find One again and fight alongside him. They could keep each other safe and Casey wasn't sure if she could do that on her own.

Without much choice, Casey opened her eyes again, blinded by sunlight. It was much colder now, but it was a comfortable coolness. Casey rubbed her eyes to clear her vision and found herself standing on the sidewalk, half a block from her house, the spot by the stop sign where she'd first met One.

One?

Casey turned in a full circle. Where had she come from? How had she gotten here? What day was it? Something faded fast from her memories and she couldn't put a finger on it before it slipped away. The sudden loss of memories created a vacuum inside her head and she dropped to her knees on the sidewalk, panting. She was home, but where had she been? What did home even mean?

XXV

ONE

Motionless, One schooled his breathing like he'd trained himself to do in tense situations. He inhaled slowly to control the frustration starting to eat through him like a lazy fire. The deep, bellowing laughter echoed through the connected dimensions, making One want to end the communication right then. If he had any better options, he might have.

One knelt in the center of the pentagram, head bowed, arms held rigidly at his sides. The circled star shape in the luxurious flooring was an elegant violet that glowed like midnight. The entire space looked elegant, but One knew it was all for show. Around him lay an office, looking human in nature, some potted plants, surely fake, next to a window with the curtains shutting out nonexistent sunlight outside. The wood desk looked human as well aside from the fact that it would be taller than One if he stood up. The demon in the oversized chair was large, both vertically and horizontally, dressed in a mock suit, like his intent was truly to discuss business with One.

The fat, snake-eye demon seated behind the desk was still One's best shot so he waited for the joke to stop being so funny.

"Amazing," the demon wheezed. "I never thought a human could get herself into so much trouble all on her own. You see everything working this job, I swear. Dealing with paramortals all day is exhausting but the stories I hear... Amazing."

One muttered through clenched teeth. "That's not the point. It goes against our established codes for a demon to steal a trader's bounty whether or not they were the one to commission the target."

The official picked a nail of his pudgy finger, still smirking. "Okay, I'm sorry to hear that a rogue angel — famous for not following rules — didn't follow a rule. I'll make sure you get reimbursed for the blood you would've made on the sale."

One didn't move an inch, still glaring at the demon behind the desk. The respectful head-bowed posture he was supposed to maintain had been lost. With the uncomfortable restlessness that had formed in One's stomach, it took intense willpower to keep himself on his knees. "I can't take that offer. It's your job to protect soul trade. I don't want reimbursement; I want to deliver the mortal to my client."

The amused grin fell off the demon's face. "It's just a job. If I give you what you want, you should go away. You're bleeding on my floor."

Theoretically, the offer of recompense should've been

enough to satiate One's request and he wondered how much further he could push this case before it got suspicious. One wouldn't be selling Acacia once he got her back. If it was the last thing he did, One swore to return her to her home, safe.

It was a mess, really. One never should've gotten attached to a mortal; he knew the consequences firsthand of getting too close with someone who would die so soon. One shouldn't have told Acacia his story or let her inside his realm. He should've let her die a casualty of the Holy War in the former trade house or better yet, he should've stayed away from the trade house altogether when he'd felt the uneasy presence of the angel trap within. At the beginning of the day, One might've actually been able to turn Acacia in, before he started talking to her, before he started wanting to save her. One shouldn't have taken a soul trade job in the first place, should've let the other traders battle for her life. Never again.

One took a deep breath, hoping his voice didn't betray his desperation. "If this is your response to soul theft, the trade is going to fall apart. Traders are going to learn they can capture targets and not care whether or not they reach the demon who commissioned for them because they'll get paid anyway. Demons are going to learn they don't need to commission for souls; they just need to wait for the opportunity to steal one without paying for it. I don't know what 'compensation' blood you're planning on giving me or where it came from, but soon those will be the only demons contributing. There will be revolts. The system will fall apart. Is that what you want to—"

"It's just one girl!" The demon scowled.

"It is *not* just one girl." One stood up, looking the demon in the eye. "Today, maybe it is just one girl, but tomorrow, it's your entire world, the economy we operate by. Who will be to blame when this trade goes down? My guess is it'll be you, too lazy to play your part."

Eyeing One's defiant posture, the demon's upper lip twitched. "Gogmuth perished in the angel attack and for all I know, that's your fault. You don't know which demon took Acacia Wickstrom when she got away from you and I hardly think that's anyone's fault but your own." The demon seemed to change its mind and gain some conviction. "I shouldn't even be offering compensation to you. I should cast you out of my office right now! You lost the girl and that's your problem!"

One knew finding Acacia was a long shot at best, even with the investigator's assistance. The demon hive mind only went so deep and there was a lot of activity in the expansive demon realm to sort through. "She was stolen from me and it appeared that the demon that took her was waiting to ambush. It may be a demon connected to her past somehow, one that's been with her before this. When I put up the ad for her, I didn't give a location. For a demon that already has a connection to Acacia, it wouldn't be hard to find her again. That also means the demon is from around here if it's been with Acacia her whole life. Does that narrow your search?" If One was right about his assumptions, finding the perpetrating demon wouldn't be difficult for the investigator still scowling down at him from the tall desk. One stood confidently. He'd spent long enough playing subjugate to this particular celestial and his bad attitude.

Another amused grin replaced the creature's irritation. "Now I understand why you don't want compensation. With Gogmuth dead, you could auction her off to the highest bidder and walk away with twice as much as you had planned from one soul. Who's playing the economy now?"

"I'm not in it for the payment," One insisted, stepping right to the edge of the pentagram. "It's about keeping the trade alive for all of us. I won't stand for injustice like this and I don't have any hesitations about finding your superior and letting him know that it'll be your fault when the trade falls apart. I've been doing this a long time and I have a feeling he would want you to be pulling your weight — and you have quite a bit of weight to be pulling, if you'll pardon me."

The investigator's face heated with anger and he rose from the desk, glaring at One. "Okay, I'll look into it! I don't have all day to deal with petty crimes against nameless paramortals. I needed to make sure it was worth my time to investigate this!"

One stepped back into the center of the pentagram, letting his expression communicate that the respectful gesture was not backed by any such reverence.

"You'll regret talking to me like this." The demon sat down

across the desk, shaking the room. "I happen to have some information on Acacia Wickstrom already that someone notified me of earlier. I can take you to them, but that's where my involvement ends if they know where she is. Are you armed?"

"I am." One breathed an invisible sigh of relief, sliding the holy nail out of his pocket halfway, watching the fat demon's narrow eyes glisten.

Scowling again, the investigator recited the rules of entry into the demon realms. "You'll do well to keep your weapon sheathed from here on out. After leaving the circle, you are not protected from demon attack and there will be no official you can whine to when you end up dead because you whipped out an immortal weapon."

"I understand," One said, stuffing the nail back down next to the vials of demon blood.

"Good. Step out of the pentagram and follow me. I'm taking you to a seer. He will find your mortal."

XXVI

CASEY

By the bright, morning sun, Casey figured it couldn't be later than 6:30 am. The early summer sunrise was as beautiful as always, but Casey felt too sick to appreciate it. Rising from her knees, Casey took a stumbling step back to her house. Was she drunk or something? She couldn't remember how she'd gotten there and everything hurt. Had she been drugged? Kidnapped? Had she fallen while running and hit her head?

Reaching her front door, Casey fumbled with the knob, finding it locked. Her last solid memory was leaving the house for a run, but she always unlocked the door while she was gone. Everything since that time was a blur she couldn't hold onto for more than a moment at a time.

She rang the doorbell once. Her parents would wake up and let her in. They might be mad about being woken up early, but it was better than sitting outside all morning.

Instead, the door was thrown open almost immediately and Casey was met with the shocked face of her mother. Mrs.

Wickstrom's eyes were dark and smudged like she hadn't slept and her hair, curly and dark like Casey's, was a mess, sticking wildly out of a clip. Tears promptly filled the woman's eyes and not for the first time recently, Casey could tell.

"Mom?" Casey whispered, being yanked into a tight hug. "Is everything okay?"

Pulling her daughter tighter into the embrace, Mrs. Wickstrom choked on a sob. "Where have you been? Baby, I thought... I didn't know what to think."

Speechless, Casey allowed her mother to pull her inside where she was looked over by worried eyes and desperate touches. "How long was I gone?" As hard as Casey racked her brain, there were no memories to be found. She could've been gone an hour or a month for all she knew. Her stomach filled with dread. Something unnatural was happening and she didn't know what to do about it.

Mrs. Wickstrom looked skeptical and rightly so. "You don't know? A whole day, Acacia. I called the police. There's an amber alert out for you. I need to let them know you're here and safe. I didn't know what to do when I woke up and you weren't home from running. I checked with Rose's family but they hadn't seen you and neither had Dylan's. I called everyone from your track team but no one knew where you were."

Casey closed her eyes, trying to process. It made sense that if she didn't come home from running, that she would end up with one of her friends. But she hadn't been with any of them.

Where had she been? It was ambiguous, but there was definitely an ache in her heart that told her something bad had happened. Her head had cleared from when she regained awareness on the street corner, but no new memories had returned yet. Where would she go for a whole day that didn't involve any of her friends? "I'm going to lay down for a while. I don't think I feel good."

Forehead creasing, Mrs. Wickstrom grabbed Casey's arm and pulled her away from the stairs. "Where have you been, Acacia? You can't disappear like that without explaining!"

"I don't know!" Casey snapped and yanked her arm away. The stairs seemed a little too tall now, her mother a little bit too worried, the house a little too overbearing. "I just needed to get out, I guess. I needed a change of scenery for a day."

Casey's mother shrunk back. "You've never done something like this before. I wouldn't have worried if you were spending the day out with a friend. I just needed to know. I don't care what it is you did or where you went if you think you have to hide from me. I really don't care. I only want to know so I don't have to worry."

If the sick feeling rising up again in Casey's stomach was any indication of the memories she'd forgotten, her mother might not have been fine with where she'd been all day, but she had no way of knowing, no way of explaining. Maybe this was a good opportunity for Casey to show her mother she was growing up. She was in charge of her own life and could go where she wanted and didn't have to tell anyone. If she wanted to disappear for a day, she could and there was nothing her mother could do to stop her.

Ignoring her mother's protests, Casey stalked back to the front door and flung it open again. Rose's house was only a few streets over and Casey's closest friend seemed like the perfect escape from her own home, rapidly closing in on her. She'd be safe there from all the questions she didn't have answers for.

When Casey's best friend answered the door, she looked as exhausted and startled as Mrs. Wickstrom had. "Oh. I didn't know you had come home."

"I just got back," Casey said flatly, pushing her way inside. "Mom won't leave me alone. Can I stay here until I feel better? I don't want to talk about it right now but I'll be fine in a bit."

"Of course," Rose answered immediately. "But, Casey... Are you okay? You're a mess."

Casey looked down for the first time, finding herself dressed in the same blue workout top as when she had left, soaked with sweat and smudged with dirt. The skin on her arms was darker than normal with rubbed-in grime. "Maybe I could shower first? I'm fine, I promise."

Rose nodded, leading Casey upstairs to the bathroom after finding her a change of comfortable clothes.

Casey avoided the mirror, going straight for the shower, imagining how relaxing the warm water would feel, soothing her muscles and washing the lost day away from her mind. Instead, as the droplets hit her skin, Casey yanked the dial to cold, finding she felt more relaxed as she shivered. Warmth didn't feel good anymore, bringing back the queasy feeling, hinting at what she couldn't remember. Casey washed quickly and changed into Rose's clothing, encountering no one as she dashed to her friend's bedroom. She fell asleep immediately as she hit the mattress. Hopefully, her mind would be clearer when she woke up.

Instead of restful sleep, Casey's dreams were full of images that didn't make sense. She was in a building, big and empty with worn brickwork. There was something on the floor in the middle of the large space but it was blurred with black like someone had scribbled over it in black pen in Casey's mind so she couldn't make out what it was.

Her arms were twisted behind her back and she didn't have the strength to fight the hands that held her. As hard as she tried to scream, no sound came from her mouth. A stranger pushed her into the room, someone Casey knew, but couldn't place now. His blue eyes flashed, unearthly.

More than the actual content of the dream, Casey's emotions battered her heart black and blue while she slept. This stranger she couldn't remember was someone she trusted. She could feel that as plainly as the strain in her arm, twisted tighter against her back. Casey thought she might have been crying. She trusted this person, but he was holding her like he wanted to hurt her and his eyes held fire Casey couldn't combat and *still*, Casey ached to love him in her heart, still torn from betrayal.

XXVII

ONE

As One walked beside the demon, he pondered the conversation. The investigator evidently knew something about Acacia all along but hadn't wanted to share the information until One threatened him. That made One nervous. A scared demon never foretold anything good. A less experienced paramortal might be elated by the good news, but One didn't trust easily anymore.

The demon hivemind stretched across the world, making almost anything one demon knew universal knowledge, but there were just as many ways to keep secrets in a species built on lies. The investigator may have picked up some intel from the database, but it had almost seemed to One that he had started the conversation with the information already handy, like Acacia's disappearance and One's search for her wasn't a surprise.

One didn't take the demon official as the efficient type, but he wasted no time leading One out of the pentagram and through the office space, out into a corridor of dark glass, transparent on all sides and much less humanesque than the office. From the first moment, One struggled to breathe. The demon realm was deathly hot and even One's tolerance to the heat wasn't enough to keep him from sweating through his t-shirt.

The demon realm was a complicated destination with the scenery changing by region so it was hard to keep track of where anything was. When One had opened the connection with the investigator, he had no idea where the official was located in regards to the parallel realm on Earth so by stepping out of the circle, he could have been transported across the country or even the world. The landscape of dark glass wasn't a region One recognized, though he hadn't seen much of the demon realm. There were few reasons a paramortal would ever need to step inside the demon realm and none of them were good. A lucky paramortal was one who never had to step outside a pentagram during an active connection. One thought through the limited options he had for an escape plan, should he need it. There were no physical passages between Earth and the celestial realms but there were plenty of pentagrams around that could provide a link back home if needed.

Then there was the matter of the so-called 'seer' who apparently knew something about Acacia. One had never met a seer before, nor known anyone who had. He knew seers were a rare breed of mortal that had access to the demon hivemind as well as all knowledge in the universe, past, present, and future. If a seer had information on Acacia, it almost undoubtedly meant there was something bigger at work here and that made One more nervous than anything else. He wouldn't take anything at face value from here out. Not the seer, nor Acacia, nor any demon One talked to was insignificant.

Transportation through the demon realm was also tricky, One knew from stories. The seer, being mortal, had to exist in a fixed location whereas demons could easily teleport anywhere they needed to be. Paramortals, unusual visitors to the realm, had to find their own way to travel as well. Traditionally, they used pentagrams found sporadically throughout the realm and were usually required to be accompanied by a demon so they wouldn't get lost in the immense realm.

One saw the pentagram in the glass floor from a distance away, following the investigator and stepping into the large, glowing circle. The pentagram of demon origin didn't feel the same as his own, One discovered quickly, his strength being drained from his veins as the connection locked on with the demon guiding One's mind to it. One opened his eyes to a different section of the demon realm, judging by the appearance, and the investigator ushered him out of the pentagram.

This new area looked closer to the mortal world aside from the walls made of fire on either side of the hallway. A door stood open a short distance ahead and the investigator shoved

One toward it. "The seer is in there. Go complain to him about justice or whatever then get some other demon to take you back home."

With that, One was left alone in the hall made of fire. He hadn't expected much more from the lazy demon investigator, but being alone in the presence of a seer still made One question the quality of this plan. Steeling himself, One stepped through the doorway with no idea of what to expect.

"Close the door behind you, please," said a soft voice.

One hurried to comply, finding the interior of the room to be even more mortal-looking than outside with carpet on the floor and drywall on all sides, painted light blue. It was also much colder inside the room, closer to Earth temperature, clearly meant for the comfort of the seer, sitting in the center of the room.

Clearly, One's prediction of the seer was misinformed. Instead of a wizened old man with eyes that glowed, One was faced with a young boy no older than Ezra, cross-legged on the carpet with a sketchpad in his lap, the tip of his pencil gracefully pressing lines into the paper.

The boy looked up at One, smiling with perfect contentment. "Hi,"

While they didn't look anything alike, One couldn't help but think of Ezra when he saw the seer. Both boys shared a friendly disposition and the quiet sadness in their eyes of someone trapped by fate. One approached the boy, unsure how to act. He bowed awkwardly, then sat down on the floor. "You're the seer?"

"I am." The young seer smiled cheekily, fanning the pages of the sketchbook and looking at One with blue eyes under straight black bangs. "So many questions! No, I'm not paramortal, I'm 100% human. Yes, that means I'll die in the blink of eternity's eye, but seers are born in every generation, so there's no need to worry. No, seers aren't the offspring of demons and humans as far as I know. No, I am not paid minimum wage. Yes, I know the name you were born with, *One*. It's nice to meet you; my name is David."

The controlled expression One had maintained so far fell off his face. The worst thing about demons was their knack for sneaking inside minds, reading thoughts, but One could always feel the pokes and prods at his consciousness when a demon slipped inside, a sensation all paramortals were accustomed to. Sitting across from David, One hadn't felt any indication that he was reading his mind, but he'd answered all the questions One never would've asked out loud. It was an unsettling power, especially if the boy was as good as he bragged, but it could be just what One needed to find Acacia.

Giggling, David went back to his sketchbook. One couldn't see what he was drawing, but he didn't care about the seer past what One could get from him to help in the search for Acacia. The seer's expression stayed fixed in the carefree smile. "Acacia Wickstrom, huh? She's safe. I don't know what you're so worried about. She's back home where she belongs. She's with a friend right now, spending the night like the good old days."

"That's not what I need to know," One said through gritted teeth. On one hand, he was relieved Acacia wasn't dead or being tortured in the depths of the demon realm, but experience told him Acacia's life hadn't resumed the way it had been before. Whichever demon stole her wouldn't be finished until it got something out of her, most likely her soul, damned to hell for eternity. "I want to know about the demon that took her so I can ask payment for the soul I captured."

"You don't have to tell me what you need," David said without looking up from the paper. "I know what's going on in your head. But I guess if it makes you feel better, I guess you can talk at me. But I know what you're really looking for. Pride took Acacia away from you, a demon who's never left her alone. He's teamed up with Rebellion and" — David laughed — "She's not the same little girl she once was. Anyway, Pride might be a little difficult to reason with for your payment, but I'm sure you'll get what you're owed. I know how badly you need to survive so you can get back home to Ezra."

One was quickly tiring of the head games. He scowled at the boy. "Is that all or are you going to keep teasing me?"

"Manners, One!" the seer laughed, a light chuckle that sounded like any boy's should, not like One would expect from a demon-employed seer, currently trespassing in his mind. "If you're mean to me, I might demand even more payment from you!"

"What?" One whispered and closed his eyes, heart rate increasing. Of course there was a catch. Deals with demons were easy to negotiate, but this was a different game that One never should've agreed to play. He didn't have time for payments or more mind games. One needed to get Acacia to safety as soon as possible and get the demons away from her. "What do I have to do?"

The seer boy's eyes were sad and big as he looked at One. "Whatever I want you to do. Infinite knowledge comes at a price and I have a hard job. It's been a long time since I've had someone to play with. Do you think Ezra would like to draw with me?"

"No, absolutely not." One stood up from the floor, eyes narrowed. "You don't get to *look* at my brother, much less play with him. He's not even real. Find some other kids to play with if you're so lonely, but you're not getting near him."

Unimpressed, David shrugged. "Ezra's a lot more lonely than the mortal kids. He'd love to have someone to play with. He's been kept all alone in that house for decades, One... And if you don't comply, I'll have you killed and you won't get the demon blood you're owed and you won't see Acacia again and she'll go to hell when she dies and Ezra will die too and everything you've done so far will be for nothing. It's not that much to ask for. It's lucky you have a little brother for me to play with because some people who ask me for knowledge don't. Then I have to take something else from them and that's not as much fun for me anyway. We can go to your home realm now if you're ready." David stood up from the floor and flipped his sketchbook shut, still smiling. "I can't wait to meet Ezra."

XXVIII

CASEY

Dim light filtered in through the blinds when Casey opened her eyes. After a moment of disorientation, she remembered falling asleep in Rose's bedroom and the unfamiliar surroundings became clear. Unfortunately, even after sleeping, Casey couldn't remember any of the previous day's events aside from the white-haired stranger and the crippling feeling of betrayal from the dream that kept her pinned to the bed, so real that she couldn't have imagined it. Where had she been? What had her eyes seen?

The digital clock on the bedside table read just past 7:00 pm. She had slept for almost twelve hours and still didn't feel rested.

Casey crawled out of the bed and left the room. This was her best friend's house, somewhere she usually felt just as comfortable as in her own home, but today she couldn't shake the feeling like she was a stranger here.

The light was on in the master bedroom, hopefully

implying Rose's parents were inside and Casey wouldn't have to deal with concerned adults wanting to know what had happened to her. It wasn't just adults who were worried about her, Casey knew. Her best friend would be concerned too and wouldn't accept her weak excuses.

As Casey approached the landing at the top of the stairs, she didn't have time to think of a convincing lie, seeing the living room down below, occupied by Rose in her usual chair and Dylan, perched on a couch.

Both teens stood up at Casey's appearance, looking relieved. Casey placed her best smile over her lips and hopped down the stairs. She wasn't faking her excitement to see her two closest friends and knew she had their support no matter what she went through.

Dylan scooped her into a tight hug and Casey could feel the desperation and worry in the touch. She felt the slightest pang of guilt for making everyone worry and wished she could explain herself in some way to satisfy everyone. Rose joined the embrace, too impatient to wait her turn, claiming her fair share of Casey's affection.

Blinking back a few tears, Casey hugged her friends back and whispered, "Thanks, guys."

They all pulled away at the same time, Rose returning to her chair while Dylan helped Casey sit down on the couch next to him, keeping a hand on her back. He brushed a piece of long, dark hair behind Casey's ear with a familiar gentleness Casey loved. "What happened? We were all worried about you."

Casey shrugged. "I don't know what came over me, but I needed to get away for a bit. Maybe it's because we're going to be seniors and I'm excited to forget about all the dumb rules of being a kid. I wanted to see the world with my own eyes for a while and see where life was going to take me."

Rose frowned and crossed her legs. She didn't look satisfied. "Your mom thought you had been kidnapped when you didn't come home from running. I just talked to her too, she was worried you'd been drugged. You acted so strange when you came home. I didn't disagree with her. You are acting weird. I called you a hundred times yesterday and you never picked up.`"

"Lost my phone," Casey admitted, not sure why it mattered so much now that everyone knew she was okay. She hadn't thought about her phone, but evidently, she had lost it somewhere along her unknown route because she definitely hadn't had it when she found herself on the street corner. "You can lighten up a little. I feel fine. I *am* fine. I'm in charge of my own life and no one can stop me from going out and enjoying the world every once in a while."

"You're not usually like this." Rose pouted. "Have some responsibility, Casey. People were worried about you."

"Sorry then." Casey thought back over the missing day in her timeline. The story about adventuring by herself was probably a lie and the scariest part was not knowing the truth for herself. Still, she was old enough to take care of herself and nothing bad had happened. She was still here and fine and everyone else needed to lighten up. She was behind the wheel of her own life and she didn't need anyone trying to take care of her anymore.

"Casey, snap out of it." Rose leaned forward and rested a hand on her best friend's knee. "You didn't see yourself when you got here. You were dirty and tired and you looked... haunted. What happened to you?"

The only haunting Casey knew about was the dream that refused to leave her mind. She was back in the real world now anyway and it didn't matter, but she still couldn't stop thinking about the traitor she loved. Maybe it was a metaphor.

Rose stood up from her chair and huffed. "Are you hungry, Casey? We saved you something from dinner."

Casey nodded eagerly. Lost amongst her memories, she had no idea the last time she'd eaten; food of any sort sounded incredible.

As Rose left and reappeared with some cold pizza, Dylan continued rubbing Casey's back. He didn't look as nervous as before, but a contemplative look rested in his brown eyes. "So what did you learn while you were out discovering yourself? Were you meditating or something?"

"Don't be ridiculous," Casey scoffed around a bite of pizza. "You know I'm not religious."

Dylan shrugged, looking embarrassed. "You said the other

day that you were kind of Christian. That seems like a kind of Christian thing to do, you know? You go out and seek somewhere quiet and pray or something."

"I'm not really Christian," Casey insisted, rolling her eyes. "Just because I used to go to church as a kid doesn't mean I pray or feel like I have to follow the rules or anything. Personally, I like to believe I'm in charge of my own life.[35] Look, I get it; what I did was reckless and I won't do it again since it stressed you guys out so much, okay?"

Frowning, Rose took a step toward the stairs. "I'm going to tell my parents you're okay. They were worried too."

Casey sighed and finished the last bites of dinner, surprised at how fast she'd eaten, even considering how hungry she was. She looked over at Dylan, offering a smile. "Are you mad at me too? It seems like everyone's mad at me for this."

"I'm not mad," Dylan promised, leaning down to give Casey a quick kiss.

The gesture felt wrong somehow and Casey frowned, pulling away. She couldn't decide how she felt, if the kiss was too much or not enough, or just plain wrong. She didn't know what reason she would have for feeling like the kiss was wrong so she leaned into Dylan, hoping that would make her feel better.

Dylan traced a hand up Casey's arm. "I'm just relieved you're okay. Do you want me to walk you home? Your mom came over earlier this afternoon to check on you but you were still sleeping."

Casey shook her head, pressing her body close to Dylan's. "Maybe we could go to your house or we could drive your car somewhere where it's just the two of us alone. I want to spend time alone with you."

The teen boy pulled away from the touch, looking surprised. "You never want to be alone with me. You always prefer group dates even when I suggest going out alone."

"Please, Dylan? I was soul-searching, remember? I want *you*. I don't have words to describe how much I love you. Maybe you feel the same way?"

Dylan's eyes narrowed and he stood up from the couch. "Casey, no. I don't know what you're thinking right now, but I don't like it. I love you, but you always said we were just for fun, that our relationship might not ever be serious, but just for someone to cuddle with or whatever! You've never been like this, Casey."

"Don't you think I'm entitled to ask for a change in what we are, though?" Casey stood up as well. "I know what I'm doing and we don't have to listen to anyone else's rules to do what we want to do. I know what I want, Dylan. Don't you?"

"Please stop," Dylan begged, backing up to the front door. "We can talk about this another time but I can't say yes to this right now."

"I thought you loved me." Casey's head wasn't in the present. She wasn't even thinking about Dylan, directing the words to some abstract being in her subconscious.

"I do love you," Dylan promised firmly, his tone growing colder. "But the answer is no. I'm going home. Talk to you later, Casey."

"Then you're betraying me too!" Casey yelled after Dylan as the door slammed shut. "I hope you're happy!"

Rose bounded back down the stairs at the sound of yelling, her eyes searching Casey for an explanation. "What's wrong?"

Casey felt her defenses crack under the weight of everything she didn't know. She ran back to her best friend and cried. "It feels like everyone I love is betraying me and I don't know what I'm thinking or feeling but I know it's wrong and I don't understand what's happening to me! I used to be happy; I don't recognize who I am now. What happened?"

Shushing Casey, Rose pulled her toward the stairs. "It's okay. No one's going to betray you, least of all Dylan. Stay the night here if you want. I know you just woke up, but you can come hang out in my room with me. I don't know what you need, but I'll do my best, Casey."

"Thanks," Casey sniffed, appreciating everything her friends had done for her, yet somehow still feeling like it wasn't what she wanted.

XXIX

ONE

While One hadn't necessarily been looking forward to babysitting duty, he found only dread when David cheerfully told him he wouldn't be hanging around while he 'played' with Ezra. It made One nervous, leaving his brother alone with the creepy boy.

David held his sketchbook against his chest, standing in front of One. "I'm ready to go."

One scowled and touched the boy's shoulder. It felt wrong to place a hand on the unsettling seer, but he didn't have much of a choice. He released David promptly as he appeared in the entryway of the house.

"That's a cool trick." David's smile never wavered. "Not everyone's demon powers are that cool."

Biting back a snappish comment, One watched the amusement cross David's face as the jab was received anyway. Maybe his chosen power was 'cool' but at least some paramortals had useful abilities instead of One's that just reminded him of the boy he'd failed to protect when he was mortal.

Alerted to the noise of entry, Ezra stepped out of his bedroom and stood at the top of the stairs to watch the front door, his eyes wide at the sight of the other boy. Aside from Acacia, David was the first person One had let into the house in over a decade.

"Alright, One, you can leave," David said, strutting inside and looking around, his gaze falling on his new companion. "Hi, Ezra. I'm David and I'm going to play with you today."

One clenched his fists at his sides. This wasn't safe for Ezra, he was almost positive. It wasn't worth the snippet of information he'd gotten about Acacia and One desperately wished he would've known the terms and conditions of the contract first.

"There's a lot of shiny stuff here," David commented, picking up some of the heavenly gold off a table. "You're a good treasure hunter, One."

Ezra looked at One with confusion, asking the question with his eyes.

One shook his head slowly. Ezra couldn't see the heavenly relics. Ezra wasn't real. David was probably going to spend the day ruining Ezra's fictional life here, revealing all of One's secrets, even the ones that didn't need to be shared with anyone, much less Ezra.

"Why are you still here, One? I said you could go." David

walked toward Ezra, still smiling. "Do you like to draw, Ezra? I love drawing. We're going to draw in your room."

Meeting Ezra's eye one last time to hopefully communicating love and regret, One turned back toward the front door and left the two boys alone. He'd never left Ezra alone like this before.

Instantly, he was back in the demon realm and One let his fury out from behind the dam, punching the nearest wall, watching paint crackle and drywall crumble. David would be able to see this and he would probably be mad about it, but One didn't much care what David thought anymore. At the end of the day when One took David back to his proper realm, it would be the last time they saw each other and One would never deal with a seer again as long as he lived.

Until the end of the day, One needed to occupy himself somehow. He wanted to start investigating Acacia and the demons of pride and rebellion that had infected her, but it would be a challenge to get back to her via the pentagrams in the demon realm. One didn't know exactly where he was in the world and he could lose himself for eternity without proper direction through the portals. Asking a demon for help was the only safe way to travel down here but that meant the risk of owing another favor. One was done owing favors today.

He would be stuck here all day and that was probably David's idea all along. One didn't like being useless when there were things that needed to be done. Acacia needed to be saved and so did Ezra. And yet, One was trapped in the seer's part of the world, frustrated and totally useless.

One turned his attention to the room, wondering if there was anything valuable he could look at or steal. If the seer was going to have his way in One's home, One didn't have any hesitation doing the same in return. He tipped back a vial of demon blood, taking another dose and hoping it would make him feel a little better as he waited for this hellish day to end.

There were very few possessions in the small space for One to even go through. He supposed as a seer, David had all the information he needed in his head and working for demons, he probably didn't play with toys like a normal child his age.

Instead, stacked against a wall was a collection of sketchbooks like David had been drawing in while talking to One. There had to be at least a hundred of them, One estimated, approaching the stacks with some curiosity. He hadn't bothered to look at what the demon slave had been drawing earlier, but the contents of these sketchbooks could be valuable and unless David stepped back into this realm to stop One, there was nothing to interrupt his snooping.

The book One picked up first was full, each page drawn on with the precision of a professional artist. The papers were full of sketched faces, some mortals, some demonic, some paramortal, some angelic. Almost all had a note written in the lower corner, commentaries that made One sick to read.

Beneath the detailed drawing of an old mortal woman,

David's scrawl read, 'About time she met her end! Ha ha!'

With a picture of a muscular demon with teeth like a boar, 'He smells like rotten eggs but don't tell him or he'll sit on you! He's sensitive about that!'

One threw the book on the floor, satisfied when some of the pages bent. The kid was seriously messed up, One concluded from the drawings. It didn't make him feel any better about leaving Ezra with a psychopath. If David was mortal though, One could easily skin him alive with the crucifix nail once he returned to his home realm. Seer or not, David could still bleed.

Giving the discarded book another satisfying kick, One picked up another, flipping open the cover. He startled at the image on the first page, an uncannily accurate depiction of his own face, his eyebrows slanted with rage and his lips pulled back in a snarl.

The note at the bottom read, "One, it's been cool getting to know you! You weren't on my radar at all until I saw you in my future. I think you'll find yourself somewhere interesting soon! Also, it's very rude to look at people's sketchbooks, don't you think? Ha ha!"

Breathing hard through his mouth, One flipped the page, finding a picture of Ezra, once again, very accurate for a subject who hadn't seen the light of a real day in decades. This note from David read, "Thanks for letting me play with your brother! I'm having a *great* time! You'll have to excuse the bruises — I didn't want to hurt him but we can't have people fighting back, right? Ha ha! Don't try to come back to your realm until the end of the day or *someone* is going to get in trouble!"

One closed his eyes, concentrating on controlling his anger. The little brat was playing off his fears. There was no way to be sure Ezra would fight back or that David would hurt him. The seer was full of himself and loved to brag, but he was a filthy liar and One wouldn't be tempted. He turned the next page of the sketchbook, hoping for another smelly demon or dead grandmother.

Instead, he was met with a beautiful sketch of the Ark of the Covenant, light gleaming off the gold exterior of the box. 'Wow, One, you helped steal the Ark! That's very cool! Too bad everyone on your team betrayed you!'

David was still showing off. Anyone with access to relic hunter data could find out One had been part of the team to successfully find and steal the Ark of the Covenant. The seer was just trying to get under One's skin and he would rather stab himself with the crucifix nail than admit it was working.

The next page made One's blood run cold. The picture was of Acacia — of course it was. Her face was peaceful, eyes shut in sleep. She was pretty in her peacefulness, a form One hadn't seen her in before, always scared or angry or desperate in the time they'd spent together.

'She's beautiful isn't she, One! Too bad you had to care

about her! Don't think the big bosses will be too happy about that, huh? Going soft for a mortal? I thought you were cooler than that! You should know better than most why it's a bad idea to mess with mortals, right? Sucks about the scar on your face; it's really ugly! Ha ha! I don't think you'll get out of this without another scar or two either.'

At its mention, the raised white line under One's eye tingled and One resisted the temptation to touch the old injury, the lasting result of the last soul trade job he'd worked and the reason it had been over eleven years since he'd gone after anything but treasure. It was a constant reminder: he was prone to going soft on people and Acacia was proof again of his weakness.

David's note continued. 'Don't worry, you won't have to admit you like her because I did it for you! I told the demon in charge about you. He's sending guards over to arrest you right now! (Thanks for letting me use the pentagram in your basement. It was cool to show Ezra how to use it too!) Who *knows* what kind of punishment you'll get for trying to help a mortal escape! If I get to help decide, I'll make sure it's something really bad! But don't worry, I'll keep my promise and I'll leave your realm at the end of the day so you don't have to worry about me doing anything bad to Ezra while you're in demon jail! Ha ha! Thanks for coming to talk to me today, One! It was *really* cool to meet you!! -David'

One dropped the book, already running for the door. With

impeccable timing only possible for a seer, the door opened milliseconds before One reached it, allowing access to two demons. Both were humanoid but mutated from their original angelic form with feathers and patches of fur over their bodies.

"I can explain!" One yelled, backing away quickly. "You shouldn't listen to whatever that little seer kid told you; it's not true! I didn't do anything!"

The guards ignored One without acknowledging the protests, grabbing his arms and dragging him from the room, sketchbooks left open on the floor.

XXX

CASEY

Casey could almost make believe that she was having a normal sleepover with her best friend, where they both sat on the bed, eating snacks and gossiping. Rose hadn't touched the orange slices she'd prepared but Casey devoured them, still feeling empty on the inside. It was late and Casey could see Rose getting tired. She prompted her best friend to go to bed instead of trying to stay up with her.

"You sure?" Rose looked embarrassed. "I know you just woke up so you don't have to sleep or anything. I feel bad for leaving you alone though."

Putting out the lamp, Casey laid down next to her best friend, offering a shaky smile. "It's okay. I'm still exhausted, honestly. I'm pretty sure I'll be able to sleep if I close my eyes."

Rose seemed satisfied by that so Casey left the issue alone, rolling over to face the wall so Rose didn't have to see her eyes, still wide open. Casey wanted to sleep and feel rested, but she didn't want another dream she couldn't explain. She didn't want to wake up feeling alone and betrayed again, a nervous rock in her stomach to weigh her down. Still, the pull of the darkness worked quickly, taking advantage of the busy day Casey couldn't remember, dragging her back to where she couldn't control her thoughts.

Daylight welcomed Casey when she opened her eyes and sat up abruptly. Despite the extra six hours, she didn't feel chipper like she usually did in the mornings. Rose was still next to her, clutching a pillow and breathing quietly.

Casey tried for silence as she crawled out of the bed, but Rose shifted and opened her eyes when the bedroom door creaked open.

"Morning," Casey said. "I'm going out."

Rose was up in an instant, joining Casey by the door and rubbing her eyes. "I'm coming with you then. Are you going running?"

The full weight of darkness descended on Casey and she leaned against the door to steady herself. She should be going out running; it was what she did every morning. Yet, it was the last thing on her mind now. She'd woken with the burning pain of betrayal in her chest, accompanied today by the desire to do something about it. Some of the images were clearer now, the warehouse downtown, the pentagram on the floor. She had to see this place again, had to know what had happened. Not knowing was going to drive her insane otherwise. "I'm going downtown. There's something there for me and I'd like to go alone."

Rose placed herself between Casey and the door, arms crossed. "Hell, no. I don't want you to go anywhere by yourself." A silent 'because you might never come back' hung in the air as both grabbed their shoes by the front door and headed outside.

Neither said a word as Casey led the way, following half-formed memories and intuitions down streets and out of the neighborhood. The light rail station was only a mile away and already bustling with people making the commute to work in the city. Casey hadn't brought the money required to buy tickets, so Rose covered it, still keeping silent, but watching Casey with blatant caution. Casey wanted to say something, prove that she was following a real lead here, but she didn't know what to say. It wasn't like she needed to prove herself. She hadn't asked Rose to come with her and she would've found her way alone.

Boarding the train car, Casey felt drawn to the back row of seats. A businessman in a nice suit sat there today, checking his phone as he waited for the train to move.

With abnormal confidence, Casey approached the man, looking down at him with arms crossed. "Can I sit there?"

The man looked up, confused and irritated. "There are plenty of open seats."

"But that's *my* seat."

Rose grabbed Casey's arm and pulled her away before any more damage could be done. The blonde smiled at the businessman apologetically. "Sorry, sir! Don't mind her!" Rose led Casey to a different row of seats, heaving a sigh as Casey stared at the back bench seat. "What is your problem?"

Casey's eyes shifted to the back of the train car. A window in the doorway showed a glimpse into the back compartment of the car, full of electrical equipment. "Hold on," Casey whispered, stepping back to the end of the train car and wiggling the door handle. It was locked so Casey pulled harder at it until a hand landed on her shoulder.

"Ma'am is there a problem here?" said the stern voice of a stewardess. Every eye in the train car was focused on Casey as she tried to break into the restricted car and was led back to her seat by the worker. She sat in silence for the rest of the trip, ignoring their looks.

Disembarking the train, Casey pulled Rose through the crowds of the city, through a plaza that looked strangely familiar and down streets that should've led her where she wanted to go. Instead of the warehouse in her dreams, Casey found a hundred buildings like it, but none of them correct. Casey wandered deeper into the city slums, most of the buildings here abandoned or for sale. Rose was complaining about being arrested for trespassing or getting jumped by a gang and Casey was starting to get irritated.

"Casey, I don't even know what we're doing here," Rose protested, backing away from another building with dark windows. "I'm starving and it's getting hot and we should go home. I texted my mom where we were going, but your parents are going to get worried—"

"Let them be worried!" Casey burst out, all her built-up frustration exploding. "I don't know what the hell I'm doing! Maybe I'm going insane because the building from my dream isn't here and I'm chasing phantoms and I don't know what's happening to me!"

Rose backed away slowly, holding her hands out in caution. "It's okay. We'll figure this out, right? Let's go home, please?"

Numbness sinking in, Casey followed Rose back down the narrow streets toward the train station, boarding the same light rail they'd taken down. It was less crowded this time and Casey saw the back seat open, rushing to sit down by the window, a view she knew she'd seen before, in some moment lost to her memories.

Inexplicably, tears flooded Casey's eyes. She turned away so Rose wouldn't see.

Her best friend saw anyway and brushed back a piece of Casey's hair. "What are you looking for, Casey? Let me help if I can, please."

"You can't," Casey insisted, picking at the seat cushion. "I'm not sure if what I'm looking for even exists or if I'm going insane."

XXXI

ONE

As soon as the demon guards grabbed One's arms, his instinct was to jump back into his home realm and wait out the danger. Even if it went against David's orders, One was more equipped to deal with the little seer than the two massive guards. One had been itching to stab the kid anyway. One closed his eyes and willed his body into the separate dimension, but nothing happened.

Heavy cuffs closed around One's wrists, the metal bands laden with runes One didn't recognize. When he looked over his shoulder, a guard smacked him to face forward, a painful reminder of his place in the hierarchy.

One figured the cuffs had something to do with his inability to jump realms, and he struggled against the hold. Of course, David would be smart enough to take measures to prevent One from jumping realms, having foreseen this moment and everything about to happen.

Allowing himself to be dragged along, One stepped back

into the pentagram outside with the demon guards. It looked vastly different from the glass halls and corridors surrounded by flames that One had seen so far, instead made up of stone. The pentagram was located on the outer edge of a large stone temple, lost to time and rot. Demons walking over the uneven ground rubbed it smooth. The corridors through the tunnel were dim but lit with torches and the faces of deities were carved into the rock.

The hall opened into a vast chamber, ornately carved with a tall ceiling. On the far side, a massive throne sat against one wall, holding the largest demon One had ever seen.

Demon hierarchies were simple in their structure. Ranks never changed, staying the same as they were at the time of the Fall. More powerful demons almost always had higher ranks and their size reflected their status. Regions of the world were ruled by the higher ranking demons. They did as they pleased as long as they stayed within standard demon rules — not a hard feat when the rules only called for as much destruction as possible.

One was shoved to his knees in the center of the large throne room, as the massive demon looked down on him with contempt.

"This is the traitor," one of the guards said, jabbing One in the side with the dull end of the staff he carried. "Just as the seer said, we found him destroying things in his chamber."

The large demon was quiet for a moment. "Look at me."

Before One could move to obey, the guard to the left dug its fingers into his hair, wrenching his head back to look at the regional overlord.

"Do you fear me?" the massive demon leaned forward, clearly aiming to intimidate.

It worked. "Yes," One whispered, his voice echoing in the vast chamber. "Only a fool would underestimate your power."

"I am Moketh, king of this region." A twisted smile split the demon's face. "You are wise to respect me."

One had never been in the presence of a regional prince. He looked around the throne room without moving his head. The dark and ominous appearance of the temple reflected Moketh's personal style but One didn't know how to use that knowledge to his advantage. Torches burned along the walls, casting large shadows. One squinted into the darkness, sure he saw the shadows dancing as they shouldn't. A clawed foot shot out and One realized that the shadows along the edges of the room were full of smaller demons. A couple crawled out of the darkness, glancing at Moketh every few seconds as they skittered across the floor toward One, sniffing cautiously at the uncommon presence of a paramortal in the throne room. Not typically invited into the demon realm, One hadn't encountered these pests before either.

Moketh saw One's wandering eyes and smiled. "Don't mind them, halfling. They can't hurt you. They're barely sentient. They serve no one but the urges of death and mindless destruction.[36]"

A small demon, only half One's height pushed closer, hissing quietly at the guards before poking at One's hand and dashing off again, expecting a result. One kept perfectly still, stuck on his knees with the guards' hands on his shoulders as more of the small demons crawled around, investigating the intruder. The feeling of the small demons' claws was sickening and uncomfortable as they made a game of exploring One, tugging at the sleeves of his t-shirt, untying his shoes, yanking on the belt loops of his jeans until one tore off. They all scattered in temporary terror, only to crawl back seconds later to continue the game.

One tried to keep emotion from his expression and look steadily at Moketh. Since being captured, One kept in mind the single best chance he had for escape. The arrest had been made hastily and the bloodlust of the crucifix nail in One's pocket was reassuring.

A minor demon stuck its hand down the back of One's shirt and he jerked away, making Moketh laugh at his evident discomfort. The pressure of the guards' hold decreased and One needed no other prompting. He shifted and pulled his legs through his bound arms for more mobility, grabbing the holy nail from his pocket as he whirled around. The two guards were the first to fall with black, tar-like goo pouring from their bodies as they died at the tip of the immortal weapon. Most of the low-level demons fled the scene but One managed to slice the slowest few in half first.

Moketh's expression barely shifted, but he motioned with his hand and dozens of demons raced out from behind the shadow of the throne. Most of them were at least twice One's height and he bolted for the door of the throne room, aching for cold, clean air of freedom again.

The demons caught up, tearing claw marks in One's t-shirt as his shoulders were recaptured. The door was only feet away and One pulled against the mob of guards to reach it. Instead, he was heaved against the solid, stone surface of the door, the air effectively knocked from his lungs. One was lifted back by several pairs of hands, then slammed against the wall again, this time on his back so when his vision cleared, he was met with the snarling expressions of the guards. So close.

In a last-ditch effort, One swung the nail in front of his face wildly, taking down one of the guards before his arms were pinned above his head by a taller demon and the nail was wrenched from his grasp. One closed his eyes, preparing to be dragged back to Moketh when a sudden bolt of pain tore a cry from his mouth. One glanced up to see the crucifix nail impaling the center of his right hand, sticking out of the stone door. Blood, slow and thick with added demon essence trickled down to his shoulder as the wound throbbed and the demon guards stepped away to enjoy the first-class entertainment of suffering.

One couldn't pull against the nail without sending fresh

waves of pain all through his body. He kept perfectly still but had to bite back screams. Immortal weapons and paramortals didn't get along and One could feel the demon blood in his veins protesting the holy nail as it kept him stationary against the wall.

The faint smile on Moketh's face hadn't changed, though it blurred in and out of focus as One struggled to stay upright. "Take the traitor to the dungeon. Secure him so he can't disappear to his own little universe."

The nail was torn back out of One's hand and he screamed again, collapsing instantly to his knees, only to be hauled upright again by the demon guards and marched from the throne room.

After too many flights of stairs, the dungeon lay before One.

The cells blurred and tipped in One's light-headed vision. They were sturdy in construction but far from pretty, made of stone and iron bars. Shouts and screams echoed around the room, though One couldn't make out any words. The cell he was pushed into was small and cylindrical, the diameter barely big enough to sit down in. Carved into the floor and ceiling were mirror images of the same pentagram, filled with runes and symbols. The door clanging shut made the bars of the cell vibrate and One dropped to his knees again, feeling sick with pain and hopelessness. The cuffs had been removed now that the designs of the cell prevented him from escaping. One sat on the floor for an indefinite amount of time, clutching his right hand to his chest while the other prisoners, mostly monsters and demons, roared and shook the ground with protesting stomps. The nail had gone straight through, One found, inspecting his hand, finding ragged flesh and snapped bones sticking through the skin on both sides.

The doors to the dungeon opened several times through what One figured was a day and each time, he rose to his feet, hoping and dreading it was someone coming to deal with him. When the time did come, One saw David approaching with several large demons, looking perfectly content as always, like nothing phased him. The boy hung in the back of the group, reminding One that the seer didn't hold as much power as he gave him credit for. David was still mortal and the demons didn't answer to him. The sight of his gentle smile still reignited fury in One's chest.

The troop of demons stopped outside the cell and the lead pressed his piggish face against the bars, glaring at One. "Mortal sympathizer. Do you forget your place, halfling?"

One stood in the center of the cell, trying not to flinch away from the rotting smell of demon so close. "I did not help a mortal escape. Acacia Wickstrom was stolen by a rogue and I'm trying to make sure justice is enforced so soul trade doesn't collapse."

"The seer claims Acacia Wickstrom has memories of kissing

you."

One froze. He didn't remember that and he wouldn't have allowed that to happen either way. David looked serious but One couldn't be sure he wasn't lying. "I never kissed a mortal. If... If she did anything to me it was when I was unconscious from loss of demon blood and that's not my fault."

"You were weak from a shortage of demon blood for a time, correct?"

"Yes."

"Could that have softened your heart toward her? As you lost your powers, you may have empathized with her suffering and allowed your mortal side to take control of your actions?"

"No, sir. I have plenty of demon blood on hand and I can assure I'm doing the same job as always, or I would be if you would let me go so I can bring her in." The interrogation wasn't going anywhere, One was sure. No good conclusions would be reached from the discussion. The mind-reading abilities of the demons and David would reveal that One had hoped for Acacia's escape.

"On your knees." A second demon approached the cell with a small glass cup in hand, sloshing with black liquid. "If a lack of demon blood softened your soul, we'll see if this fixes your shortcomings. Know who owns your soul, who you fight for in this war."

One protested but the demons had opened the cell door to lean inside. The first held One's mouth open while the second poured the demon blood down his throat. One screamed, though it didn't help the pain. A drop or two at a time was the limit for any paramortal and this was at least a hundred times more. No paramortal was meant to handle so much demon blood at once. It raced through One's system, entering his bloodstream almost instantly, oppressing his mortal functions as it went, leaving him curled up on the floor of the cell, writhing in agony.

The demons didn't leave yet, instead poking their way into One's mind, planting images of Acacia being tortured, dying, being torn apart to create a new paramortal soul like One's. As hard as he shut his eyes, One couldn't escape the pain of torment, all the tactics of hell raining down on him.

The beating sensations of the demons' assault lessened after a while and One lay still, listening to the pounding of his own heart like thunder.

A shifting sound on the stone outside the cell opened One's eyes a crack. He saw David, standing over him, a thoughtful expression on his young face. "I had a great time with Ezra today. Thank you, One."

One tried to swear but his mouth wasn't working, nor any part of his body.

David knelt down. He glanced over his shoulder at the few remaining demons outside, his escorts, talking amongst themselves and not paying attention to the cage. "One, I can see everything that is and will be, but that doesn't mean the future is set in stone. It changes constantly before my eyes and I don't know what decisions will lead to what outcomes any more than you do. I work for demons, but that doesn't mean every future I see is in their best interest. When I look at you, I see your future shift. It's interesting to watch and wonder which of those futures will be your reality. The future I saw for you first was what got me interested and what makes you such an important prisoner to the demons. I still can't tell if you will spend eternity here with your future in flux as it is. That worries the demons, but it's very interesting to me. I've never seen a paramortal escape hell before, never seen it as a possible future for someone. They thought if we hurt your family, hurt you, and imprisoned you here, it would solidify the future, but I still can't see it clearly."

David stood up again, glancing at One before walking away. "Escaping hell for all eternity would be pretty cool, don't you think?"

One lay still, watching David walk away with his escort. The words were too much to process. He closed his eyes, only able to hear the roar of pain.

XXXII

CASEY

The scenery flew by the train window as Casey watched. The events of the day were already piling up and it was like opening her eyes for the first time on what she had been doing. She'd already managed to find trouble on the train and wandering the slums downtown and it was incredibly lucky she and Rose hadn't gotten into any trouble. Casey wasn't sure who she was before or who she was now or how she had changed, but she didn't think she liked the results her new self brought about. She didn't know who to blame for a shift in her entire personality, from someone who loved life to someone only making things harder for herself.

Casey tapped three times on the window, knocking on nobody's door and whispering, "I'm going insane."

"You're not going insane," Rose stated from beside, touching Casey's shoulder. "You're just going through a hard time. Talk to me so I can help you."

"I can't. I can't talk about what I don't remember. It's

feelings mostly and none of them feel good." More tears came to Casey's eyes as she picked at the seat cushion on the light rail train. "Last night I wanted to sleep with Dylan and I've never felt like that before. I think I knew he was going to say no, but what if he hadn't? What's wrong with me? Sometimes I feel like I have no idea what's important in life. All I do is run and pretend like that does anything for me. Maybe I won't do track next year. There are so many more important things to think about and do in the world than running in circles."

Rose kicked the floor under the seat. "Then I feel sorry for you. I thought this life wasn't so bad. I don't think it's bad to enjoy what you have."

"I don't either!" Casey argued, shutting her mouth again after that, offering a silent apology for snapping. "I can't shake these thoughts though, like everything that used to matter just isn't that important anymore. Maybe I've outgrown worrying about parents or school clubs. I'm better than that, right?"

"I don't know," Rose shrugged. "If banging your boyfriend is what you care about now, that's fine. If that's what you call living, be my guest, but I would never want that life. Maybe you are better than what we have now. Maybe you're better than me if I'm still happy with this."

Casey leaned against the window and sighed. "I feel guilty for thinking that. But I don't know how to change my thoughts."

"Maybe you're too good for this life, like you said." Rose

crossed her legs. "I hope you find what you're looking for."

Exiting the train when it pulled into the station, Casey split off from Rose, each walking separate paths to get home. Casey's heart ached to fix the new gap between her and her best friend, but she didn't know what to say. She didn't even understand her own life well enough anymore to know how to mend a relationship with someone else.

Casey realized as she turned onto her street, that this would be the first time seeing her family again since leaving her mother alone and frightened in the entryway the first time she'd tried to come home.

It was the hottest part of the afternoon and Casey knew she still looked upset, dressed in Rose's clothes with her hair unkempt and her skin tinged red from the hot day running around downtown looking for ghosts.

She came downstairs for dinner, awkwardly quiet and empty of conversation. Casey could've talked about going downtown with Rose, but there were no highlights of that trip to embellish. Across the table, Mrs. Wickstrom caught her daughter's eye for a split second, then hurried to look away. A pang of guilt shot through her heart. She had done this to her mother, hurt her and made her worry more than she should have to.

Anger rose up where guilt had been and Casey clutched her dinner fork. It wasn't her fault her family looked miserable. She wasn't controlling their emotions. They were just miserable people and Casey wasn't about to let that stand in the way of where she was headed. She was more than this life and the misery of lesser people wasn't going to hold her back.

That feeling didn't sit well in Casey's stomach either and she excused herself from the table, retreating into her bedroom to stare at the ceiling.

All around her were running posters and countless trophies and medals from track meets. The message was clearly written for her, she just hadn't seen it before. Track wasn't even competition for her anymore since she'd pulled ahead as the fastest on the team and no one could rival her. She was too good for this life, her family, her friends, her boyfriend who didn't even seem like much of a prize anymore.

Casey rolled over, clutching a pillow. She was scared to fall asleep and meet the stranger in her dreams again, feel the unstoppable race of her heart as she chased him, never to catch up, always to be let down.

This night's dream was worse than the previous and Casey sat upright, breathing hard, new sunlight streaming in through the windows. So much pain. Casey had felt all of it in her heart and wondered what it meant. Maybe it was the stranger's payment for betraying Casey. Maybe he deserved what he got, but it didn't help Casey feel any less sick to her stomach.

Casey sat huddled against her headboard until a soft knock

on the door announced Dylan's arrival. She welcomed him in, grateful she hadn't scared him off for good. Without a phone, Casey couldn't contact anyone, but her boyfriend knew, as he always did, when she needed him anyway.

The conversations between them that used to be so easy had left, keeping them both straining for something to agree on now. Casey felt like any time she responded to Dylan, she was saying the opposite of what she should say. She was almost positive he was going to leave and give up on her for good soon. They just weren't the same couple anymore, innocent with the dreams of high schoolers filling their minds.

But instead of leaving, Dylan turned the TV on, staying with Casey all day without creating anymore awkward situations in conversation. It was comforting, having him there and Casey felt a little more vulnerable at the end of the day when he left to return home. And yet, with Dylan gone, she was free to think the thoughts she wanted, that had been hiding all day behind a desire not to rock the boat anymore.

The thoughts weren't good, of course, but they were what came when Casey closed her eyes.

Another dream came and went and Casey woke up in tears, shed for a stranger she loved and hated. Dylan came over again, bringing Rose with him and they all sat and watched TV without saying much all day. Casey was still grateful for their presence, keeping all the feelings she couldn't explain locked away until nightfall.

The rest of the week proceeded the same way, but Casey could only wonder how long Dylan and Rose would keep coming over, only to get nothing out of her aside from a smile that hopefully communicated that Casey was still trying to feel better. With the time spent together, some of the tension eased. At least they could talk about TV without bringing up too many tough topics. But every night, Casey was left alone to brave another silent family dinner where no one knew how to talk to the new version of her and another deafening night alone with her thoughts. She felt like she was starting over again, incapable of becoming who she used to be.

It had been a whole week, Casey realized, sitting at the dinner table on Sunday night. Last Sunday morning she had gone out for a run and reappeared on Monday morning without her phone, her memories, and another key part of who she was, lost to mysterious circumstances. A week had gone by and she hadn't rediscovered what was missing yet.

Dylan had stayed for dinner and it was the closest Casey had felt in a long time to how things used to be. There was some light conversation around the table and Casey found herself laughing at a few jokes, though she didn't dare speak up and risk saying something wrong. Maybe she could pretend to be who she was before, even if she didn't feel the same. The old Casey had been so much happier and she couldn't help wanting that back after spending dinner with a smile on, forgetting about the stranger in her dreams and the change of her disposition.

The dishes were soon cleared and Dylan threw his shoes on by the door, arms outstretched for a goodnight hug. Casey was happy to fall into the embrace, leaning against Dylan's shoulder until his arms squeezed too tight around her back and a wave of claustrophobia pounded into her heart.

Casey pulled away abruptly, willing her hands to stop shaking and her heart to slow back down.

"You okay?" Dylan murmured, ducking his head to look into her eyes. "What's wrong?"

"I don't know," Casey whispered. "Too close. Sorry."

Hurt flashed across Dylan's face as he stepped back. He chuckled nervously to cover it up. "So the other day you wanted to sleep with me, but now I can't even get a hug?"

Before a single cohesive thought made its way through Casey's mind, her hand shot out and she slapped Dylan across the face, eyes narrowed. Rage from somewhere unknown built a fire in the pit of her stomach.

Eyes wide, Dylan backed away, touching his cheek. "I'm so sorry. I shouldn't have said that. I'm sorry, Casey."

Casey glanced over her shoulder to the kitchen, hoping her parents hadn't noticed anything going wrong in the foyer. "I'm sorry too. I'm trying to feel better, but I don't know what's going on. I'm trying to be who I used to be, but it doesn't feel right. I'm sorry for the pressure it's putting on you, but I don't know what to do!"

Dylan exhaled. "I know. I'm sorry. Is there anything I can do for you?"

Every emotion in Casey's heart still felt mixed up and she couldn't hold onto anything for more than a second before it left her mind again. Sometimes she thought she knew what she wanted, sometimes she wanted Dylan, and sometimes she wanted something she couldn't even put her finger on. "Say my full first name."

Confusion replaced Dylan's expression. "Acacia?"

Casey's heart sank. It still wasn't right. Dylan's tone or his voice in general or the way he looked at her, *something* wasn't right and Casey was frustrated with turning over clues only to find dead ends. She was chasing something but it didn't appear to be waiting for her. "Never mind."

Dylan's hand landed on the doorknob and he sighed again. "I hope you get through this, Casey. I'm running out of ideas of how to help you. Call me if you still want me around, I guess."

As Dylan left without another attempt at affection, Casey couldn't help feeling like he was making an excuse to escape. She retreated to her bedroom without a word to anyone else. She'd been spending a lot more time pajama-clad in her bed lately, staring up at the ceiling, sheets in a pile at her feet as the warm summer night made its home in the humid air settling over everything.

Instead of fighting sleep like usual, Casey invited it tonight, stuffing her face into the pillow. It had been a full week now since everything had changed and she felt awful that she had spent it feeling conflicted, in a limbo of not knowing what she wanted while she displeased everyone around her. She hated the nightmares she'd been having all week, filled with pain and suffering. She felt it as clear as her own, but after the awkward goodbye with Dylan, she just wanted company, even if it was the stranger in her dreams.

XXXIII

ONE

Days slipped away and One felt every second of passing time amplified by the steady pounding of his heart, locked in the prison of his ribcage. The extreme overdose of demon blood surged through his veins like a roiling sickness that kept One on the floor of the cell.

Several times a day, guards visited the prisoners in the dungeon and One heard every word, roar of tortured pain, and argument. The demon blood made his every sense a hundred times more sensitive so every sound was a blast in his ears. It made him want to curl up into an impossibly tighter ball on the floor.

When the guards approached One's cell day after day, they shared a good chuckle. They would tease and ask if One was dead yet. When One flinched away from the noise, they would laugh again and say they'd come back when the flies arrived.

Most guards would lean against the bars of the cell as they teased and stick the point of their spear-like weapons through the gaps to prod One's stiff body. Much like immortal weapons, celestial weapons and paramortals didn't get along well either. One felt the demon blood in his veins fight like it was its own entity as the sharp tip of the demon spear pierced One's skin repeatedly. It pulled a weak groan from One's mouth and the guards would laugh as they left.

As the days passed, One felt the untreated wounds fester with infections and poison from the weapon's magic properties, much like the wound from the holy nail in his hand that he kept cradled against his chest. The hole was messy with blood, throbbing in time with the pulse One desperately wanted to stop.

After five days, One hadn't moved from the floor of the cell and hadn't tried. It was much more comfortable to stay still when any attempt at movement shot pain through his body. Even if the cell was removed, One wondered if he would stay curled up, stiffness holding his position like rigor mortis.

The guards arrived at the same time they always did. Instead of opening with a rude taunt, one of the guards jabbed his spear inside the cage, the point burying itself in One's shoulder, several inches deep.

"Get up, halfling. Boss says you get to see your brother."

One's heart rate picked up, not just from being cut, though he felt the lazy trickle of blood run down his arm, staunched somewhat by the thick demon blood. If the demons were cutting him loose, it came with strings attached, One was positive.

The cage door opened and One was dragged out onto the floor of the dungeon. He found himself stronger than he would've expected, able to kneel in front of the guards. "What's the catch?"

The taller of the two demon guards smiled crookedly. "We'll be waiting for you here when you come back. It'll be sooner than you think."

Fear took over every sense in One's body, dulling pain and sharpening his mind. Unrestrained, One could jump to his home realm and stay there forever. The only reason he would have to come back was if something had happened to Ezra.

Despite the multiplying questions in his head, One blinked out of existence without another word, eager to escape captivity. Immediately, he was kneeling on the doormat inside his house. Everything was still and quiet. During his imprisonment, One refused to consider that David could've killed Ezra — One wasn't sure if Ezra could die since he wasn't real in the first place — but he still didn't want to learn the truth the hard way.

"Ezra?" One called, standing up with help from the wall and leaving a bloody streak up the side. The excessive demon blood sharpened every movement with pain as One stumbled up the stairs, checking every bedroom and finding no trace of his brother. In Ezra's room, several pieces of paper lay on the bed, torn from David's sketchbook, featuring pictures of demons. One recognized Thastrok, the entity who had turned One paramortal drawn on one of the pages. He turned and left the room without checking for any more witty notes on the drawings.

One made his way back down the staircase and searched the ground floor, finding it empty too. He had been trying to ignore one small detail the entire time, but it was too prominent not to notice. The basement door was standing open. One never left it open.

Calling softly again for Ezra, One stepped into the basement.

Sitting in the far corner, Ezra's knees were pulled up to his chest and his face was buried in his arms.

One knelt in front of the boy, biting back a pained groan, exhaling hard. "Ezra? Look at me. I'm so sorry this happened."

Ezra lifted his head from his arms, eyes growing wider as he looked over One. "I knew the only way you'd let something happen to me was if something happened to you..." Ezra touched One's wrist, sending a faint spike of pain through the nail wound.

"Come here." One struggled not to flinch as he held out his arms for Ezra. "You don't need to be down here. Let's go talk upstairs. I owe you an apology."

The boy shook his head and pressed himself further into the corner. "I belong down here. I'm not real. David took me to see Thastrok again, the demon who talked to me before. He told me who you are and who I am.[37]" Tears began spilling down Ezra's face. "You work for demons, One! I thought you loved God! You always did before!"

"I did," One affirmed, sitting down on the uncomfortable floor. "When you... when you died, I was really upset but I never meant for this to happen. I'm trying to make the most of it now though, because I can't change the situation. I have you back and that's important to me so that's why I do the things I do."

"No!" Ezra choked. "I don't want you to be held down by me! I want you to live your life! Go back to our family. They haven't seen you in so long and they think you're dead."

"They wouldn't recognize me," One argued, closing his eyes. Ezra deserved better than this but One didn't know what to do. "Ezra, it's been twenty-five years. I don't know anything about our parents now. For all I know, they might not be alive and I'd never be able to find them if they moved."

Ezra clasped his hands over his ears and screamed. "Find them! Stop making excuses! You messed everything up and you need to fix it! Acacia's still in danger and you need to save her too! I don't want you here with me so just go!"

As Ezra unfolded, One could see dark spots of bruising on his arms and the base of his throat. Anger at David rose up in One's chest again but he was angry at a lot of other things too. He was angry at Ezra, even though he was yelling nothing but the truth with his eyes shut tight so he didn't have to look at One.

One stood up and fled the basement, resting against the front door before heading back out. He did still need to save Acacia and there wasn't anything he could do about it from here. Prison awaited him back in the demon realm, but it was at least a little closer to the goal. One would never be able to look Ezra in the eye if he backed down from this fight.

A fleeting intrusive thought laughed in One's face as he opened the front door. The guards had been right. One would be returning sooner than he had thought.

XXXIV

CASEY

The stranger awaited Casey in her dreams like always, reaching a hand out for her to take. She didn't want to take the hand he offered though, feeling betrayal lingering in her heart from the last time she'd trusted him.

Casey kept waiting for the moment when she'd fall and he wasn't there to catch her, but it never came. Her guardian angel had let her fall once before, but wasn't about to let it happen again. Casey held on. He was sent to save her and she was sent to save him, no matter what it would take. There was so much to save, their futures bright before them.[38]

A new presence found its way into Casey's mind and she explored it, wishing for something to help her. It was a good feeling this brought, though she still wasn't sure what it was. The more she turned it over in her mind, the more she realized she was holding onto a miracle. She had a power that she'd forgotten about. She could fight demons and summon angels with a single prayer. Staring her in the face, it was hard to believe she'd forgotten about it for a week, but she had been blind then.

Casey sat up in bed, only the earliest rays of sun trickling through her window, encouraging her as she pushed the blinders away and found what she'd been searching for all week: her purpose, her faith, and the knowledge that she had the power to save One.

Dressing quickly, memories flooded Casey's head, reminding her of who she used to be before the day of stolen memories. There were demons with her, she knew, and she did her best to push them away as she fled her house. She didn't have any sort of plan for rescuing One. Casey didn't know all the rules, but she didn't think she could just walk into the demon realm, take One, and leave.

The morning was already warm. Casey stood still in the driveway for a moment, letting the sun warm the bare skin of her arms. Under normal circumstances, she might be returning about this time from her daily run and her body ached to fall back into the routine. She promised herself she would run again when this was over, noting the relief that found her as she rediscovered the motivation she'd always had. She could still go back to who she was before and reclaim her old titles.

Without a concrete plan, Casey walked along her normal route, hoping the morning would inspire her as always. There were more people out this late in the morning and Casey looked at them all, hoping something small and insignificant would bring her an idea. By the time Casey turned the last corner of her route, Casey hadn't come up with a plan and she wandered a bit longer, praying for something. Anything.

If the roles were reversed and she was the prisoner, One would know exactly what to do, how to navigate the demon realm and push away the entire demon army to save her. Who was Casey to think she could measure up to that on her own? She didn't have any special weapons in her arsenal[39] and she certainly didn't have experience or status to flaunt. Casey remembered fragments of knowledge she'd picked up with One, noting the main goal of demons was to capture human souls. If she could come up with no other plan, Casey thought she might be able to trade her freedom for One's. She still didn't know how to fight a demon, but maybe she would come up with something once she was fully immersed in the situation.

A figure in the distance stopped Casey in her tracks. Exactly where she'd met him the first time, the person leaned against the stop sign with casual ease, hands in the pockets of dark pants.

Casey broke into a run, afraid to blink and find a mirage. As she got closer, she thought she should be feeling joy, but dread filled her stomach instead. Something wasn't right. Her mind jumped first to the clothing. The One waiting for her at the street corner was wearing a t-shirt, the same he'd been wearing when Casey had been separated from him. The real

One would be freezing cold on Earth. Casey slowed her pace, skeptical of this One. Was it possible she was seeing another mirror realm version of him? The memories weren't complete, but Casey remembered stepping through the reflective wall into a totally new world. Her One would've found something warmer to wear before coming to see her if he had somehow managed to escape the demons.

A block away now, One turned and walked away, ducking into a side street as Casey ran after him. There weren't many places to hide in the spacious neighborhood. And yet, there was no sign of One. Maybe a mirage or a love-struck delusion had been the only thing awaiting Casey on the street corner after all and she was no closer to saving anybody.

Spying something on the ground, catching the sun's rays, Casey ran back to the stop sign and knelt. Placed neatly on the pavement was a glittering gold necklace with a blue pendant. Choking on air, Casey reached up to touch her throat where the gemstone had once lay. With shaking fingers, Casey picked up the necklace, almost falling backward as a powerful thought shot through her head.

Put it on when you're ready to find me.

The voice belonged undeniably to One, but the inflection was all wrong. Casey stood and lifted the necklace in front of her face, watching sunlight sparkle off the sides of the sapphire. Her heart screamed to put it on immediately, having found the key she needed to get back to One. At the same time, she felt hairs on the back of her neck stand on end from the second she'd touched the necklace. Each tiny gold link of the chain was warm to the touch with hell's fire. One wasn't safe and neither was she. That hadn't been her One, leaning against the stop sign, free to come to her like all was well in the world. He was still in danger and Casey needed her plan of attack quickly.

Casey fingered the delicate chain, shifting her feet. She focused and more memories came back, the finer details of what had happened to her. She remembered the other paramortals, the sandwich One had stolen for her, the shapeshifting trader the angel trap, sitting on the edge of One's bed and watching his blue eyes fill with tears as he confessed to the life he'd been imprisoned by. The tiny part of Casey's heart still worried about being betrayed was quickly smothered. After all One had done for her, it was time Casey repaid the favor.

She lifted the necklace to fasten around her throat when the sound of her name froze her.

Rose was jogging toward her from the direction of her own house, looking confused. The blonde slowed to a walk in front of Casey. "I was going to come over and see how you were doing today. Dylan told me you guys had a disagreement last night."

Casey stared at the necklace still clutched in her hand, unable to take her eyes off it. "There's something I have to do today, Rose. I remember what happened to me and there's someone I have to save. I don't know if it's going to work out well, but I have to try at least."

"I don't like the sound of that." Rose took a half-step forward. "What are you holding?"

Casey held the necklace against her chest, meeting Rose's eyes as her own filled with tears. "One gave this to me as a gift but right now it's proof that he needs help. I'm the only person who can help him even if it means sacrificing myself for his sake."

Rose frowned. "I don't know what you're talking about, but it doesn't sound good. If this is someone you love, why would he ask you to sacrifice yourself for him? And... if you're going to do something reckless, please don't do it alone. Let me help or something,"

"He's not asking me to do it, but I want to and I have to." Casey started to fidget. Something didn't feel right yet. "I'm the only person who can help him because—" Casey trailed off and realized the flaw in her plan all along. After everything she'd learned, she'd been about to make the same mistake she'd been making her entire life.

She looked up at Rose, a smile stretching across her lips — the first real smile all week. "Rose, thank you. Me and my stupid pride thought I could do this alone but I can't. I can't do anything alone and I had to let go of that to see the truth![40]"

"What are you doing..." Rose took a step after Casey as she

turned down the street.

Bouncing on the balls of her feet, Casey took quick steps away from the street corner, feeling lighter than air. "I'll see you later, Rose! I'm going to find help!"

"What are you doing?" Rose stood frozen on the street corner.

"I'm going to save One!" Casey laughed, taking off at a dead sprint. "But first, I'm going to find a church."

XXXV

ONE

Opening his eyes, One found himself back in the dungeon, the guards still standing there, awaiting One's return. They made no move to recapture One and One made no effort to flee. He knew he wouldn't get far anyway. One looked between the guards with poorly concealed fury. "Take me back to Moketh. We need to talk."

The guards cuffed One's hands, chuckling. "How's your brother, little halfling? Has he been getting along okay this week without you?"

One refused to respond, walking with as much pride and posture as he could force his aching body to maintain. There had to be a way to get Acacia back from the demons haunting her life. If One didn't make it out of this cursed realm, it was probably what he deserved anyway. But as long as he could save Acacia, he would die a little happier. Whatever it took, One was ready to do it. The guards' compliance in taking One to the regional leader was evidence that One still held at least some standing. Whether or not he was a rumored mortal sympathizer, One had been a successful soul trader until now and in a society where value was placed on achievement and usefulness, he might have some authority.

The best plan One could think of was to remind Moketh of his worth as a trader and the waste it would be to kill him without offering a second chance. After One was sure he wouldn't end up tortured in a prison cell again, he could start forming a plan to rescue Acacia. If he succeeded, there was no way back into paramortal society and he was as good as dead already, but it would all be worth it if he could do something right in his life for once.

Brought back into the cavernous throne room, One was shoved into a kneeling position, his head bowed in grudging reverence in front of Moketh. From the sides of the chamber, soft chittering noises stood out to One's ears, hypersensitive with demon blood. The pest demons recognized him and a few had already stepped out of the shadows to see the mysterious person back again in their throne room.

"Still alive, I see," Moketh spoke from the throne, voice booming.

One lifted his head to look at the ugly twisted features of the overlord. "I plead innocent of my charge." The echo in the chamber made One's voice sound louder than it was, fortunate, since his throat still burned with disuse and demon blood. The guards weren't keeping as close a watch on One, confident he wouldn't be escaping any time soon in his current state. Some of the small demons had approached, hesitantly reaching out again. They were probably scared from last time, watching their friends get slashed to bits but tempted to resume their game.

Moketh hissed, drawing One's attention back onto the throne. "You have questions. I sense them. You want to know about our ruling, why we tortured you for your actions?"

"No." One waited for the echo to fade. "I know what you find disappointing in me. I am not as strong as I could be. But thus far, I have been successful in my jobs regardless and I wish to prove my worth to you. I will bring you Acacia Wickstrom without hesitation. Allow me to go after her and I will show you I can be trusted."

"You desire a second chance." Moketh grinned, the corners of his lips stretching almost across his entire face. One couldn't help thinking it was messed up that the biggest smiles he'd ever seen were on the faces of demons. Maybe it made sense, since all the pain and corruption in the world fueled their pleasure and there was plenty of that to go around. Moketh leaned forward in his throne, looking amused. "You bring Acacia Wickstrom here and we let you go, resuming your life as a treasure hunter. That's the deal you want to make?"

One shrugged as best he could with his wrists bound behind his back and his entire body aching. "All I want is to serve again as I did. An unfortunate circumstance got in my way, but I'm sure the misunderstanding can be forgotten if you'll let me go after her."

"Permission granted to go after the mortal."

One tried not to let surprise show on his face. After the accusations and troublesome past week, gaining the demon's trust back shouldn't have been an easy task. One had a list of arguments stored in his head he'd thought up on the way from the dungeon to the throne room, a hundred compelling lies to convince Moketh of his trustworthiness. But Moketh had agreed at the first request. Either Moketh was much less intelligent than his title should suggest or there was a catch. One waited in silence for the strings attached to become clear.

Moketh inspected the claws on one large hand. "If you pardon my skepticism, I'd like to send you with an escort to be sure your intentions align with mine."

Exhaling softly, One nodded. The catch didn't sound hard to get around. Even with an escort, it was One's best chance to save Acacia by far. One could grab her and jump into his personal realm again. That would make Ezra happy and she would be safe from the demons. From there, One could wait out the drama here and figure out the rest of a plan to bring Acacia home safely without any stray demons tagging along.

Interrupting One's thoughts every few seconds, the low-level demons had resumed their game of pulling at One's clothing. There were new holes in his shirt from the prison guards' weapons the tiny demons seemed to like, poking at the injuries in various stages of poor healing. The feeling of clawed fingers on his skin wasn't any more appealing now than before and One gritted his teeth looking up at Moketh.

"You agree to my conditions of sending you with an escort?"

One bit his lip. He was far from confident about the plan, but it was the best offer he was going to get. "Yes, but—"

Moketh held up a hand to cut him off.

"Yes," One said. "I agree."

Moketh was grinning again.

"But how do you intend to send me with an escort?" One blurted. "Demons can't have a physical presence on Earth. That's why you need paramortals in the first place. I want to earn my place back, but I don't know what you want me to do."

"I appreciate your willingness to cooperate," Moketh said as if he hadn't heard any of One's protests. "Believe me, you won't have to worry about your escort getting in your way at all. It was very nice of you to so easily allow this. Have they found it yet? Oh, there they go."

A small demon lifted the back of One's shirt, finding the black anti-possession rune etched into his skin. Before One could react, claws tore bleeding lines of red through the design, breaking the image and rendering it ineffective.

One gasped and reached instinctively for his pocket but found the crucifix nail absent. All at once, the demon presences vanished from sight and One collapsed on the hard ground, the demons exploring the new body they had to inhabit. One watched helplessly from inside as a few more hesitant demons emerged from the shadows and joined, their essence merging with One's in an impact that made him twitch as he curled in on himself on the ground, the sound of Moketh's laughter above him.

One had never been physically possessed before — few paramortals suffered that fate — and it hurt worse than he could imagine. Each of the demons taking up a place in his body pushed One's own soul out of the way to make room like they were trying to physically fit another body inside his own with every new demon taking up residence. There were at least ten, if One's mind was functioning well enough to count, even with the demons' thoughts inhabiting it as well, thinking about destruction.

"You will bring Acacia Wickstrom to me," Moketh said, his voice sounding garbled to One's ears, full of the sounds of the smaller demons' shrieking. "She believes she is in control of her own life, that she needs no God. You are the idol she desires and she will not hesitate to come back for you and commit herself to us forever."

A demon stepped out from the shadow of the throne, about three times One's height. The creature looked down on him with scorn and dropped something on the ground in front of One before merging with his being as well. The new demon was tangibly more powerful than the others and took control quickly, pulling One's body to his feet. Before, One had barely been able to stand on his own, but with the demons, it was like having an entirely new reserve strength stored up.[41] And it didn't feel good.

The large demon knelt swiftly to pick up the object tossed on the floor. One felt dread seep through him as he recognized the gold necklace with the blue pendant he had given Acacia. He was helpless to do anything as the large demon took complete control and left the room.

One felt like he was watching through a hole in a box as his body moved without his permission, the large demon's intentions taking the forefront of his mind while the smaller entities continued screaming and scratching at One's soul. One watched in forced silence as he emerged from the demon realm and walked through the neighborhood to the stop sign where One had first met Acacia. He dropped the necklace on the ground, waited for the girl to appear, then quickly moved out of sight and returned to the demon realm, the trap set.

XXXVI

CASEY

The church Casey had attended as a kid was about two miles away and the nearest she knew of. She ran there, leaving Rose on the street corner to wonder. After a week of little activity, it felt great to get her blood pumping again. Two miles was no problem for her and she prayed aloud in gasping breaths as she ran, apologizing to God for trying to solve things on her own and asking for the demons in her mind to be taken from her.

Almost at once, Casey felt a weight lift from her back and she ran faster, leaving the neighborhood and tearing down suburban city streets toward the church.

The building was deserted, not a surprise for a Monday morning, but it was miraculously unlocked and Casey slipped inside, breathing hard. The hallway doors were closed and the lights beyond them were shut off, but the doors straight ahead to the sanctuary stood open, welcoming her inside. Only a few lights lit the space, shining from the ceiling every few feet and illuminating a wooden cross at the front of the room.

In the quiet dimness, the church felt so different from what Casey remembered it to be from her childhood. In all the services she'd attended, the rows of pews had been full of people, their hands raised as a band played worship songs onstage. The messages had been long and dull, Casey had always thought, and rarely had anything to do with her. She understood the principles of Christianity, to love others and love God, but there were so many other things talked about that hardly seemed necessary to her. Week after week, the minister droned on about healthy relationships and living as God would want. Casey didn't think she needed that, being the good person she was. She certainly wasn't murdering anyone so she was probably good in God's eyes.[42]

As a child, the sanctuary was full of people and voices and singing, but it had been empty for Casey's heart. Pride closed off what she needed to hear and drained the minister's words of meaning. Standing in the center aisle now, Casey stared at the cross. A verse was inscribed on the front wall, "And he sent them out to proclaim the kingdom of God and to heal. - Luke 9:2" Casey almost cried. She had seen this verse every week for years but it had meant nothing to her in her isolated faith. It was clear now that it was there for her sake. She was never intended to walk alone.[43]

Casey closed her eyes and dropped to her knees on the floor. "Be with me," she whispered. "Don't let my demons win.

259

Help me save One."

There were a hundred other things she needed to say, several years worth of prayers she'd missed out on. She crawled to the altar, head bowed and hands held out as she prayed, the reality of her situation finally sinking in. Hell had written its name on her heart and she'd condemned herself with her lack of faith. Casey cried out everything on her heart, every desperate plea to save her life and One's. The longer she sat the lighter her heart felt, held aloft with new freedom. She cut the ties with who she had once been until she finally broke loose from it all.[44]

The last week had felt empty, with no desire to do the things she loved, but now, Casey found something even better: a reason, a purpose, a calling.

Having poured every emotion from her heart, Casey lifted her head and pulled herself to sit in the front pew. A Bible lay on the seat beside her. She picked it up, turning the thick book over in her hands a few times. She needed a way to fight the demons and rescue One from the demon realm. The necklace clutched in her hand was her transportation, but she didn't have a weapon against them. Casey thought back to the night she'd spent talking to One in his house and the apparent power she had to fight demons with God's help. He had said demonic influence, like the Holy Spirit, was a matter of choice. Casey had already seen that earlier in the day when she'd prayed for God to take the demons from her mind. She had felt better immediately.[45]

Casey remembered enough from her Sunday School days and a bit from pop culture to know demons could be cast out of people because they feared the name of Jesus. She didn't need a magic weapon like One's holy nail to kill a demon in a single blow. The word of God would be her weapon.

The verse stenciled on the wall caught Casey's eye again. "And he sent them out to proclaim the kingdom of God and to heal. - Luke 9:2"

Casey opened the Bible and read the chapter, smiling. She had the authority to cast out demons in the name of Jesus. She chose God. The demons would never be able to touch her again.

The gold necklace burned insistently in Casey's hand. She inspected it again, sensing the surrounding aura of danger. Taking a deep breath, she unhooked the clasp and fastened it around her neck, feeling the heat of the pendant against her chest as she vanished from sight, dropping into the demon realm.

The stone temple stood before Casey, looming high above her. Much closer, two demons stood as if they had been expecting her. Pride's dark eyes glared, though he stood still, waiting for Casey to make the first move. Beside him, Rebellion hid in the shadow, sneering and clicking his teeth together.

Casey faced them evenly. "Take me to One or get out of my way."

Pride's eyes narrowed. "You come alone, unaided. You have learned nothing and still underestimate us. I will be your downfall."

"No, pride will not be my downfall," Casey said, almost smiling. "I've learned the error in my ways.[46] Maybe I'm the only one standing in front of you, but I'm not alone and I never will be again."

Rebellion darted forward, red eyes flashing. "Stupid girl! You're here to rescue your little crush, but you will be destroyed a hundred times before you even get there!"

Casey hid the shaking of her hands as she answered. "You two will be getting out of my way then. I appreciate it." She stepped onward, holding her breath, sidestepping around Pride and Rebellion so nothing stood between her and the looming temple.

"You can't refuse me." Pride looked perplexed that Casey had managed to pass around him. Rebellion had lost whatever clever words he had. The larger of the two demons stomped and shook the ground. "I have unfathomable power over your weak human mind and my roots run deep within you. You may think you're free, but you aren't. I'll be back."

"And when you try to come back, I'll remember I have God on my side and I'll get rid of you again. I can and will refuse you as many times as I want." Casey walked onward, not breaking her stride. "You have no power unless I give it to you. I choose to refuse you and I forbid you from influencing me in the name of Jesus Christ.[47]"

When no haughty answer met her, Casey looked over her shoulder. Pride and Rebellion were gone, just as she had commanded.[48] With growing confidence, Casey stepped inside the stone corridors of the dark temple. Immediately, she was met with a hundred demons, all facing her. She had been expected, but she hadn't been expected with a whole new arsenal of weapons. Casey stepped forward.

XXXVII

ONE

When the deed on Earth had been completed, the demons brought One's body back to Moketh's throne room. The large demon who had taken control of most of his actions fled his body and left One slumped on the floor in front of Moketh. The smaller demons had dominion again and let One sit up slowly, painting portraits of death and chaos in his head.

Moketh smiled faintly. "Did you enjoy Earth, halfling? It was gracious of me to let you see your little mortal friend one last time. Most don't get such kind treatment from me."

"Let us kill the halfling fool." The words tumbled out of One's mouth before he could force his mouth shut. His voice sounded raspy and strained, not his at all, echoing through his lips as the demons used his voice as a speaker for their own thoughts and cravings for death.

"Not now," Moketh chided. "Let the traitor feel the consequence of his action first."

One struggled against the demons, trying to take control of

his voice again, but managing little more than a strangled grunt.

Moketh looked bored. "Let the halfling speak."

The hold on One's voice was released immediately and One took a few gasping breaths. "Why? I don't understand. Why not just kill me?"

"I could," Moketh stated. "But I'm a sore loser and I'm not taking any chances. I don't appreciate being tricked and I'm not about to risk a loss. Your little friend, the seer, told me some news that unsettled me greatly. He told me the future for you and Acacia is not set in stone. I could win or I could lose my grip on you both. I do not take the seer's words lightly and I will do what I must to ensure the sun sets today with both you and the mortal in my hand. I have a feeling Acacia Wickstrom will walk straight to me as long as she knows I have you. She's in love with hellspawn, you know, and that's a very powerful motivator. Tragically for her, she can't leave you to die and you know that. Once I have her, I may let you die. You are so tired of living, aren't you."

The minor demons were at play again, choking off One's air so he could only manage a few shallow sips of oxygen. They laughed, taunting One with images of his own death, his own body sprawled lifeless on the ground. The spirits loved it, loved the image and the feeling of death and One enjoyed it too, in turn. If this was the happiest ending that awaited him, he could settle to dream of death.

One was bothered by Moketh's words. The prophecy of uncertainty sounded much like what David had told One while imprisoned in the cell. He didn't understand how his own soul could be saved, already committed to hell for eternity. More importantly, Acacia's spirit hung in the balance. The events of the next day would determine her fate, but One was steadily losing hope, foreseeing Moketh keeping a close eye on him. One couldn't do anything to protect Acacia like this and Moketh was right that she would come, only to land in this trap where One was the bait. In One's mind, there was little hope to get out alive or save Acacia from a worse fate. But then what had David seen to contradict that? What outcome could possibly result in a happy ending?

"Is David still around here?" One gasped, pushing the demons out of the way long enough to speak.

Moketh shook his head. "The seer is long gone. He told me as much as he knew and I require his service no longer. Do you seek him for answers again?"

One shook his head, putting all his strength into the movement and achieving barely a twitch. "I'm done dealing with him. I want to know what this has to do with my brother. Ezra doesn't have a place in this world, and yet, David wanted to spend time with him and the guards in the dungeon released me to go talk to him. I don't see what role Ezra plays in your big picture plan unless there's something I'm unaware of."

Moketh smiled again, amused by the suffering in front of

him. The massive demon leaned forward in his throne again, taking up One's entire field of vision and sending terror through his mind as well as all the minor demons. "You search for the way out, the missing puzzle piece. There isn't one. Your brother means nothing to me and he plays no role in this battle. But he matters to you and that makes him an extremely effective torture method."

"You went out of your way to find him, just to torment me?"

"This is hell. Torment is our job.[49]" Moketh scanned over One's defeated form on the ground. "Look at you. I'm sure you could find the strength to leave this realm and find your brother at home, safe but utterly betrayed. You would take with you the demons calling you their home for the day and he doesn't want to see you like this either. You know that, don't you. You are not bound, but you do not seek to flee. You could see your brother again, but he would see what you have become and that would tear you apart faster than the demons can."

One fell silent until a demon took hold of his voice again, a ragged laugh slipping out. "Weak! The halfling concedes! Let us kill the foolish halfling, master!"

Moketh sighed. "Come closer."

One rose to his feet, the demons in full control.

Moketh pointed at the ground beside the throne. "Keep quiet and don't kill the halfling yet. Remember this body to inhabit is a privilege for you and I will not have it squandered because you were impatient to kill. He will live long enough for the mortal girl to get here."

The demons inside One were amused by the notion, playing images of Acacia, stepping into the throne room, being tortured as One had, being possessed, dying. The picture changed to Ezra, the child looking scared and alone as he called out for One. He was doomed because of One as well, falling to the merciless abuse of the demon realm.

As tight as One attempted to shut his eyes, the images never went away. He knew this was his fault and the demons reinforced it, repeating it like a mantra. One deserved every second of the torture. More small demons stepped out from the shadows to add to the mass of dark energy inside him.

There had to be at least fifty now and One's body twitched as they all fought for control. Hands shaking, One felt around on the dirty, rocky ground. The wound in his hand from the lost holy nail rendered his right arm useless as the divine power interfered with his normal functions so One reached out with his shaky left hand, picking up a sharp fragment of loose stone. The edge of it drew blood when he clutched it in his hand and the demons cheered encouragement. One deserved this, deserved all the pain he could bring down upon himself for what he'd done to the only people he'd ever loved. The demons united in this goal, lowering the sharp rock to One's leg, ripping slow and deep through his pants and the skin of his thigh.

"Again!" the demons cried out, shifting the pointed stone a few inches higher and cutting again. It was necessary. One needed to feel the pain he deserved.[50]

XXXVIII

CASEY

Sweat ran down from Casey's neck in rivulets. She hadn't missed the stifling heat of hell, the way it sucked moisture from the air and squeezed her throat shut. Then, of course, was the horde of demons standing in her way, layers deep. Beyond their ranks was a massive stone door Casey knew would be her destination whether or not she won this battle.

Still confident after her victory against Pride and Rebellion, Casey stepped boldly into the corridor, watching every demon eye turn toward her. They were a mixed-up bunch, blocking her way to the door and the ghastly figures sent chills down Casey's spine she couldn't control. They all looked human in some form or another, but mutated, every one of them different. Casey figured the strange skin tones, claws, horns and other features were a reasonable side effect of falling from heaven.[51]

The first demon to face her was twice her height, not large for a demon, but towering over Casey. The creature had a sharp nose and fine lips pressed together. Thin eyebrows slanted to show just how he felt about Casey. He spoke with serious and meaningful inflection. "You return of your own will."

Casey forced a confident smile. Free will. She had come here of free will and that was a dangerous game to play with these creatures, but she knew what she needed to do and she wouldn't be giving into their temptation any time soon. "I do. But I'm not here to save One on my own. I have power you can't hope to combat and I've chosen my side of this war so you can't touch me.[52] You'd be smart to let me through here."

A hiss of displeasure echoed through the chamber like a rising tide, the demons shifting forward as a whole.

"There is no way for you to get to the throne room without going through us!" The nearest demon lowered the stained tip of a spear at Casey, not daring to move closer yet.

Casey forced herself to step forward, pushing the spear point away. The mood in the cavern shifted to anxious irritation. She'd already struck a nerve. "I don't intend to argue with you all day. Sorry if you were looking forward to that." Taking a deep breath, Casey walked along the path, pushing through the crowd toward the door. The reek of demon surrounded her and threatened to choke her, but she breathed shallowly, keeping her eyes focused on the entrance to the throne room as she prayed with each step she took.

The demons moved back to give her space as if they had no choice in the matter. They followed her though, never giving her more than a foot of space on any side. A few reached out with clawed fingers to touch her. Casey felt the press of intrusion into her mind, several more trying to sneak back into her thoughts.

She pushed back just as hard, whispering a barely-audible prayer as she marched forward. When she paused to take a breath, fear almost overtook her. She was halfway along the corridor and surrounded by demons on every side. Each one of them was at least as big as her with personalities that ranged from the severity of a sharpened blade to raving, slobbering insanity. But none of them could touch her.

Taking a stuttering breath, Casey resumed her prayer and kept walking. The tall throne room doors were directly in front of her and she stumbled the last few feet, pressing her hands against the warm stone doors like an island found after days lost at sea.

Glancing behind her, Casey saw all the demons she'd passed. They looked at her with mixtures of fear and anger.[53] She pulled the door open and bolted inside, throwing skyward a prayer of thanks before facing the real trial.

Of all the demons Casey had seen so far, she never had to face one as large as the apparent overlord of this temple, perched atop his throne. Even without his fifty-foot height, he stood out from the smaller demons, skin as black as midnight with white patterns dotting his skin, bordering his eyes, highlighting his towering form like a skeleton on the outside.

Casey's voice didn't work for a full minute, staring in awe up at the giant demon. The clattering of claws on stone behind her finally made her turn and look at the demons she'd angered outside. She wanted to say something intimidating to the large demon, something that sounded confident, like she was in control. She was untouched and unscathed and stood before their ruler, unafraid and unhindered.

"Um," Casey gasped at the large demon. The room's echo didn't make her weak voice sound much stronger. She couldn't read the demon's expression. He stared at her, silent. "I come in the name of the Lord and I demand..."

Casey found what she was really looking for as her eyes wandered the throne room. One knelt by the side of the overlord, weak and hunched over. The distance was too great between them to tell, but the way he held himself was wrong. There was blood on the ground and more on One's hands. It had soaked into the fabric of his clothes. He watched her as if he didn't know her, unblinking and silent.

Casey felt her resolve weakening. One had saved her so many times and always acted so confident. He knew how to get out of any situation because his dark blue eyes had already seen it all. If even One wasn't a match for the demon army, Casey had invited herself into a suicide mission. She'd been expecting to find One and then escape together, but One hardly looked capable.

An unpleasant pressure ticked the back of her mind and

Casey turned. A few of the demons from outside had followed her in, hesitant but curious to see if they could break down her barriers.

"I forbid you from entering me!" Casey yelled, clenching her fists by her sides, sending up a desperate prayer and feeling the pressure subside again. She looked back at the demon on the throne. "Give me One and let us go. I've made it this far and I'm not going to give up soon. You have no power over me."

XXXIX

ONE

From within the box, One peered through the cracks and watched Acacia enter the throne room. He beat on the sides of his cage and screamed, begging to be let out.

"Acacia, get out of here!" One screamed, knowing it wasn't being communicated through his mouth. "Save yourself and get out! It's too late for me. Let me go!"

The minor demons fought harder against One, shutting down his futile cries. The sharp stone in his hand was caked with blood. It dropped to cut at the palm of his right hand, aggravating the crucifix nail wound and shaking One out of his stupor.

One let a cry of pain slip through his mouth and the demons relished it. There were far too many demons for One to battle against from within, as hard as he tried to regain control. The fight had raged all day. Every time One gathered his strength to try and kick a few demons out, he was overpowered and forced to retreat beneath the deepest layers of his being while the demons continued their game, inflicting as much pain as possible without taking One's life.

The demons rarely looked away from their ruler so One watched Moketh too. There was so much noise in his head, but he heard Acacia speak faintly, making demands that would never be met.

Moketh didn't look happy, but he hadn't been challenged yet so there was little reason for him to be angry. Acacia didn't pose a threat. The demon overlord shrugged, looking to the base of his throne where One crouched, broken and possessed by hundreds of spirits. "You'll get no favors from me, mortal. Make your God help you out of here, but if you fall, you will be mine."

Acacia nodded, like the threat didn't bother her.[54] There were demons all around her but she hardly seemed fazed as she walked slowly toward One. The fact that none of the demons had devoured her yet was jaw-dropping. He sat, fidgeting, cutting the tips of his fingers on the sharp stone as Acacia drew nearer and knelt before him.

"How are you doing this?" One wanted to ask. The demons were so close behind her, watching. "Look out! Go back to Earth where it's safe for you!"

Offering a shaky smile, Acacia touched One's shoulder. The stone fell from his hand, clattering across the stone as he trembled before her. The minor demons had paused in their torment, watching Acacia through One's eyes. Over the course of the day, more had come and none had left, totaling more than three hundred entities playing mortal for the day in One's body. They had never for a moment agreed on what to do, leaving One to twitch and shake and war with his own body. For the first time, every spirit was awed into stillness and One broke through their ranks. "Acacia."

Tearfully, she cupped One's cheek. "I'm here."

A demon from behind Acacia reached down, wrapping a long-fingered hand around her shoulder. One wanted to scream at her to go somewhere safe, but the demons had control of him once again.

Acacia threw the demon's hand off on her own, turning to face the mob. The fire of challenge entered her eyes and all the demons inside One felt the same fear.[55] The girl crossed her arms in front of the demon and narrowed her eyes. "In the name of Jesus Christ, I banish you for eternity. Do not touch me or anyone else again."

The demon winked out of existence, banished, just as Acacia had commanded.

Slowly, the minor demons fled One's body, hoping to sneak away before the powerful girl's wrath was called down upon them as well. One lurched forward. That had been his own command. It wasn't much, but it was the first headway he'd made against the demons all day.

The rest of the demons in the room backed away slowly. Acacia was banishing them out of their own realm, something that didn't happen often.

"Get out of my temple," Moketh commanded.

One looked up at the demon overlord. His wide grin was nowhere to be found. He might have even shifted in the throne away from Acacia. He wasn't any safer than his followers or the low-level entities inside One. Acacia could erase him just as easily as any other.

A shiver raced down One's back as more demons fled from his body and Acacia knelt in front of him again, lifting his chin, looking into his eyes with horror. One knew what she would be seeing, his skin dirty and torn in a hundred places beneath his clothes, his expression slack and eyes jet black with the last stubborn demons still inside.

One gave up trying to hold himself up and collapsed into Acacia's arms, closing his eyes as a wave of force hit him, the zero-gravity sensation of falling up.

XL

CASEY

When Casey had fastened the gold necklace around her throat earlier, the journey to the demon realm felt like falling. The trip back felt like a tug in her gut, like an accelerating car. Then, it didn't feel like anything. She wasn't standing on solid ground. She wasn't real, her body wasn't real, only her spirit was, like a dream, when all she knew for certain was her own existence. Respectful reverence kept her eyes closed as she knelt in perfect silence. A hand came to rest on her shoulder, strong and warm.

"Acacia."

"Father," she whispered, barely able to move her lips. She trembled, fighting against the emotions trying to choke her. "Am I dead? Will I find heaven if I open my eyes?"

"No, child. Your time on Earth is not yet complete. I intend to let you enjoy that gift a little longer. You made Me proud today with the choices you made."

Casey shook her head, content to leave her eyes shut, as

much as she longed to see where she was. "I didn't do anything. You kept the demons away from me. On my own, I would've died..."

"And instead you chose Me and you lived. It took great strength to rebuke the demons as you did. They find every crack in your armor, any reason that will let them slip inside. You allowed the Holy Spirit to create your armor against them. By choosing Me over yourself, you blocked every attack they have. The demons can only get inside if you invite them, but you invited the Holy Spirit instead.[56]"

Tears slipped from Casey's eyes. She still felt too weak to move. "I've betrayed you so many times before. Even when I went to church regularly, I never really listened. And then I stopped going and I definitely wasn't listening for Your Word then. I've spent so much of my life trying to be the god of my own fate, pretending You didn't exist."

"You stepped into that church this morning and confessed. You gave your life to Me then and that is what matters. Your sins of yesterday have been forgiven and you have been made pure and blameless in My eyes.[57]"

Casey exhaled slowly. It felt good. She felt sure of herself. It was funny, how by giving up control, she now felt more stable than ever before. "What do I do now? I want to walk your path."

"Acacia, you have been born on this Earth with the will to choose your own path as it suits you and each day the choice is yours. That doesn't change now, but I will be your guide. You are a valued part of My kingdom and if you continue to seek the Holy Spirit in your life, you will find yourself along many new paths. The Spirit will keep out every demon you encounter along the way and will guide you down the path of your choice if it is in accordance with My will.[58]"

Casey shook her head. "But what is there for me to *do*? I understand so many things now. I can't go back to a normal life. What's waiting for me there? Track, friends, family, school, it all seems so inconsequential now compared to fighting demons."

"Do not be fooled. You do not have to leave this realm to find demons. Use your gift wisely. You have encountered a truth not everyone has seen. So many believe they can save themselves, that they are the god of their own life. Strengthen your own faith in Me and help others to do the same. Start with your family and friends. You have immense power to change their lives and their souls beg to hear My Word. The same way hell sends its warriors to take My children, I send you to reclaim and secure them. Show them they can have a place with Me as well.[59]"

"I will," Casey promised.

"Stay alert. Living in accordance with My law isn't hard but it is a conscious choice as you have learned. You will find struggle against the enemy again and it will hit you harder than before as it seeks to destroy the faith you have built.[60]

Choose My way and I will be there for you."

Crying freely, Casey nodded. An incredible feeling of loneliness lifted from her shoulders and disappeared. She hadn't even known it was there. No matter what, she had someone with her and she had a purpose in life beyond herself. "I will. I will, Lord."

"I will," Casey repeated once more, opening her eyes. She found herself sitting on the cool tile floor of the church sanctuary, the spot she'd left from. In front of her, One lay in a haphazard position, chest rising and falling but only shallowly. He looked tired as he blinked, eyes still jet black. Casey watched for a moment, strangely endeared. The familiar expressions clearly belonged to One again as his own will came out from under demonic influence.

Casey knelt over him, smiling as she ran her warm fingers along his jawline and the scar under his eye, over the darkening bruises and through his white hair. "Spirits, I cast you out in the name of Jesus Christ. Leave One and never come back."

One choked and coughed and when his eyes opened again, they had returned to the familiar blue color. Tears ran down his cheeks. Casey watched a droplet fall and mix with the pool of blood One lay in. "I'm sorry," he whispered. "I couldn't protect you."

"I have all the protection I need from God," Casey

promised. "He said I was going to be safe on my path to witness to the people I love. I'm going to tell them all about the truth. I'm starting with you, One. All this time, I've wanted to save you for all the times you saved me and now I get to."

The corners of One's mouth quirked up. "Acacia, you already did that. You saved me a while ago. I was just trying too hard to fight it to let myself be saved.[61]"

Casey returned the smile, but it fell off her face a moment later as One's eyes closed and his body went limp on the floor. "No, One, wait! I have to tell you everything I learned about God and the truth! I have to save you![62]"

In the dark sanctuary, a dim light shone from the ceiling, brightening until Casey had to look away. Calm washed over her like a blanket wrapped around her shoulders. She had already saved One. Her work on Earth had already begun and One was the proof of early success. Casey rose shakily to her feet and stepped away from the body, letting the light take One's soul where he belonged.

XLI

ONE

Even with his eyes closed, One could feel the burning of angelic light. He wanted to remind Acacia not to look directly at an angel or risk going instantly blind. Acacia's eyesight was the last thing he needed to think about though.

Released from Earth, One gasped, inhaling the first breath in days that actually felt right. Or maybe it was the first breath in decades that felt right.

Opening his eyes, One saw the Earth below through a hazy layer of clouds. It was dark down below, lights paving the veins of every road, house, and building in miniature cities. Looking off at the horizon, the gentle curve of the planet took up One's entire field of vision. Glancing briefly over his shoulder, One knew where he was.

"Thank you. My life was never supposed to last that long."

The voice behind One sounded amused but not surprised. "You're not upset? You have a lot down there to leave behind."

One sat down on nothing, staring down at Earth as if

through a window in the floor. He could reach down, swipe his hand through a cloud, dangle his legs over the edge of eternity. And yet, falling was the last thing on his mind; he was secure. "It's not my choice to make. I should be asking You if You're sure I should be here. I've spent a lot of time pointed in the opposite direction."

"And even now, you are afraid to face Me."

One made no effort to move, still watching the lights of Earth down below. His voice cracked as he spoke. "Yeah. I am scared. I'm out of second chances. I should be facing an eternity of torture right now; that's what I deserve. I chose my side of the Holy War and condemned myself.[63] Don't tease me with choices I've already made. It's not this moment that matters, but the choices I made on Earth."

The patient tone edged on amusement. "I suppose I misheard all your prayers then? You weren't *really* asking for salvation? And your efforts to save Acacia, planning to hide her from the demons so she couldn't be touched? You know what you were charged with. You betrayed hell when you started fighting for Me instead. You still think you deserve damnation?"

"I do." One rested his chin on his fist. "I made the decision years and years ago when I decided to hate You. There's no coming back from selling your soul. It doesn't matter if I wanted to save Acacia because I failed and let myself get possessed."

A shiver shot through One at the memory. He slid a hand under his shirt and down his back. There should've been a ragged mark where his anti-possession rune had been slashed but the skin was smooth and unbroken. He knew if he could see it, any evidence of the tattoo would be gone as well. One picked up his right hand and flexed it in front of his face. Poison from the immortal weapon wound had shut down his entire arm over the last week, numb to sensation and unable to move. Now there wasn't even a scar and it moved just fine. All the cuts and scars from the last days of torture and the last decades of a difficult life were gone. A healthy glow emanated from his skin, several shades darker now, like it had been when he was mortal. The untidy hair that fell in One's eyes was dark brown instead of pure white.

The recreated, fake Ezra had always asked why they looked so different. One missed being mortal, when everyone had commented on how similar the Valera brothers looked. He had missed this body. He had missed being—

One blinked emotions away from his eyes. "How could You possibly love me when I became everything heaven despises? When Ezra died, I turned from You. I told mom and dad I hated You and I never wanted anything to do with God ever again. Dad was disappointed and told me that like a shepherd would leave his flock to find one missing sheep, You would find me no matter how far I ran.[64] But that was the night I was taken from home and turned into a tool for the demons. I told myself that if You would supposedly leave the ninety-nine to find the one, I would be waiting. But I was One for twenty-five years and You never found me."

"I never lost sight of you, my child, but I would never force you to come back to Me. You ran for a long time, but you deny yourself the credit you deserve for what you feel. I've heard your prayers. You knew where your loyalties lay when you asked Me to take you back and when you protected Acacia so she could be safe in My arms. You could've turned her in many times to the demons if you really wanted to but you didn't."

One blushed. "I tried. Stuff kept getting in the way but I would've..."

"I can't force you to be here. If you believe you deserve hell, that's the end of the line. But you have been faithful so you have a place here. Where will you spend eternity?"

"Ezra's here, right? I'll get to see him again? For real this time?"

"Ezra Valera is with me. And he's excited to have his older brother back. For real this time."

The sun was starting to peek around the side of the Earth, the first golden rays dancing in One's blue eyes. "It can't be that easy. Every action has consequences and I have to pay for the choices I've made. You know what I deserve. I don't want hell but I deserve it."

"As does every human on Earth."

"Let me do something to pay. I'll be a double agent and

rescue people from soul trade like I did with Acacia. It'll be dangerous, but I'll do it."

"The price for your salvation was paid when My Son died to take your sins from you and clear the path to heaven for you and every other sinner down there.[65] There's no need for you to fight anymore. Your place is here. I know Acacia would appreciate having her guardian angel watching over her again."

Tears choked off the argument One was going to make. Somewhere down below, Acacia would be seeing the sunshine of a new day. "She'll be protected?"

"She has faith. That will be all the protection she needs. She has something to believe in now and that includes you. You showed her how to believe again. Ironically, if you hadn't let her believe you were an angel protecting her from the other traders, she might have lost what little faith she had left. Even when you were operating against Me, you worked to serve my purpose. Funny how that happens, isn't it.[66]"

The comeback One prepared was lost in the sunrise as it took his breath away, leaving him with little more than a strained whisper. "Why did You let Ezra die? I keep asking that question and I never get an answer."

"Death was never a part of My plan for this Earth. You know that. But if you could see every way Ezra's death touched someone and how such a tragedy was used to glorify Me, it might give you a better understanding."

"That's not good enough." One crossed his arms. "I've heard enough about 'Your plan for all of us.' Ezra was innocent. He loved You and I loved You and our family loved You. I thought You were looking out for us because of our faith. What did we do to deserve this?"

"I have never promised a life without hardship to anyone. I have never promised following me would be easy. I simply promised that through it all, you wouldn't be alone.[67] I think you see the bigger picture in this. Ezra Valera grew up with an older brother to show him My love. And through Ezra's death, Angel Valera made it back to Me too.[68]"

One winced at the sound of his old name. A long time had passed since he'd been Angel, but he missed it. "I felt alone though. I was alone for a long time. Where were You then?"

"Right where I always was. You didn't see Me when you turned away from me, yes, but then you turned back to Me and found...?"

"That You had always been there," One sighed. "I'm sorry. I took so much from You. Wing feathers of angels, halos, the torn curtain, the crucifix nail, the Ark of the Covenant... Every relic I've stolen was a stone thrown in my anger and I'm sorry.[69]"

"You think the kingdom of heaven is made of angel feathers and torn curtains? You think every gold coin you took weakened this? Face Me, thief."

One stood, taking a last look at the slow turn of the Earth before turning to face the Father.

"Angel, the only thing of value you have ever stolen from Me was yourself.[70]"

¹ At that moment, the curtain of the temple was torn in two from top to bottom. Matt. 27:51

² When the soldiers came to the place called "The Skull" they nailed Jesus to a cross. Luke 23:33

³ As the body without the spirit is dead, so faith without deeds is dead. James 2:26

⁴ and do not give the devil a foothold. Eph 4:27

⁵ The Spirit clearly says that in later times some will abandon the faith and follow deceiving spirits and things taught by demons. 1 Tim 4:1

⁶ Those who had seen it told the people what had happened to the demon-possessed man. Mark 5:16

⁷ For false messiahs and false prophets will appear and perform great signs and wonders to deceive. Matt. 24:24

⁸ For such people are not serving our Lord Christ, but their own appetites. By smooth talk and flattery they deceive the minds of naive people. Rom. 16:18

⁹ The angel of the Lord encamps around those who fear him, and he delivers them. Ps. 34:7

¹⁰ Be strong and courageous. Do not be afraid or terrified because of them, for the Lord your God goes with you; he will never leave you nor forsake you. Deut. 31:6

¹¹ Rather, worship the Lord your God; it is he who will deliver you from the hand of all your enemies. 2 Kings 17:39

¹² The wages of the righteous is life, but the earnings of the wicked are sin and death. Prov. 10:16

¹³ Do not be anxious about anything, but in every situation, by prayer and petition, with thanksgiving, present your requests to God. Phil. 4:6

¹⁴ In speaking of the angels he says, "He makes his angels spirits, and his servants flames of fire." Heb. 1:7

¹⁵ They drove out many demons and anointed many sick people with oil and healed them. Mark 6:13

¹⁶ You believe that there is one God. Good! Even the demons believe that—and shudder. James 2:19

¹⁷ Everyone who calls on the name of the Lord will be saved. Rom. 10:13

¹⁸ But let all who take refuge in you be glad; let them ever sing for joy. Spread your protection over them, that those who

love your name may rejoice in you. Ps. 5:11

[19] For God so loved the world that He have His one and only Son, that whoever believes in Him shall not perish but have eternal life. John 3:16

[20] For the wages of sin is death but the gift of God is eternal life in Christ Jesus our Lord Rom. 6:23

[21] For it is by grace you have been saved through faith—and this is not from yourselves, it is the gift of God. Eph 2:8

[22] But the Advocate, the Holy Spirit, whom the Father will send in my name, will teach you all things and will remind you of everything I have said to you. John 14:26

[23] Truly I tell you, people can be forgiven all their sins and every slander they utter. Mark 3:28

[24] Even if they sin against you seven times in a day and seven times come back to you saying 'I repent,' you must forgive them. Luke 17:14

[25] Then you will know the truth, and the truth will set you free. John 8:32

[26] For you took my silver and my gold and carried off my finest treasures to your temples. Joel 3:5

[27] What good will it be for someone to gain the whole world, yet forfeit their soul? Or what can anyone give in exchange for their soul? Matt. 16:26

[28] and that they will come to their senses and escape from the trap of the devil, who has taken them captive to do his will. 2 Tim. 2:26

[29] Then Peter came to Jesus and asked, "Lord, how many times shall I forgive my brother or sister who sins against me? Up to seven times?" Jesus answered, "I tell you, not seven times, but seventy-seven times." Matt. 18:21-22

[30] to open their eyes and turn them from darkness to light, and from the power of Satan to God, so that they may receive forgiveness of sins and a place among those who are sanctified by faith in me. Acts 26:18

[31] This is the confidence we have in approaching God: that if we ask anything according to his will, he hears us. 1 John 5:14

[32] Watch and pray so that you will not fall into temptation. The spirit is willing, but the flesh is weak." Matt. 26:41

[33] Pride goes before destruction, a haughty spirit before a fall.

Prov. 16:18

[34] For rebellion is like the sin of divination, and arrogance like the evil of idolatry. Because you have rejected the word of the Lord, he has rejected you as king. 1 Sam. 15:23

[35] In his pride the wicked man does not seek him; in all his thoughts there is no room for God. Ps. 10:4

[36] When he arrived at the other side in the region of the Gadarenes, two demon-possessed men coming from the tombs met him. They were so violent that no one could pass that way. Matt. 8:28

[37] What a person desires is unfailing love; better to be poor than a liar. Ps. 116:11

[38] Know also that wisdom is like honey for you: If you find it, there is a future hope for you, and your hope will not be cut off. Prov. 24:14

[39] The weapons we fight with are not the weapons of the world. On the contrary, they have divine power to demolish strongholds. 2 Cor. 10:4

[40] The one who sent me is with me; he has not left me alone, for I always do what pleases him. John 8:29

[41] For he had often been chained hand and foot, but he tore the chains apart and broke the irons on his feet. No one was strong enough to subdue him. Mark 5:4

[42] But where can wisdom be found? Where does understanding dwell? No mortal comprehends its worth; it cannot be found in the land of the living. Job 28:12-13

[43] For we live by faith, not by sight. 2 Cor. 5:7

[44] For you have been born again, not of perishable seed, but of imperishable, through the living and enduring word of God. 1 Peter 1:23

[45] If you believe, you will receive whatever you ask for in prayer. Matt. 21:22

[46] When pride comes, then comes disgrace, but with humility comes wisdom. Prov. 11:2

[47] And these signs will accompany those who believe: In my name they will drive out demons; they will speak in new tongues Mark 16:17

[48] Submit yourselves, then, to God. Resist the devil, and he will flee from you. James 4:7

⁴⁹ They will throw them into the blazing furnace, where there will be weeping and gnashing of teeth. Matt. 13:42

⁵⁰ Night and day among the tombs and in the hills he would cry out and cut himself with stones. Mark 5:5

⁵¹ For if God did not spare angels when they sinned, but sent them to hell, putting them in chains of darkness to be held for judgment 2 Peter 2:4

⁵² You, dear children, are from God and have overcome them, because the one who is in you is greater than the one who is in the world. 1 John 4:4

⁵³ The seventy-two returned with joy and said, "Lord, even the demons submit to us in your name." Luke 10:17

⁵⁴ The Lord will fight for you; you need only to be still. Ex. 2:13

⁵⁵ He shouted at the top of his voice, "What do you want with me, Jesus, Son of the Most High God? In God's name don't torture me!" For Jesus had said to him, "Come out of this man, you impure spirit!" Mark 5:7-8

⁵⁶ For the Lord your God is the one who goes with you to fight for you against your enemies to give you victory. Deut. 20:4

⁵⁷ so that you may become blameless and pure, "children of God without fault in a warped and crooked generation." Then you will shine among them like stars in the sky Phil. 2:15

⁵⁸ But when he, the Spirit of truth, comes, he will guide you into all the truth. He will not speak on his own; he will speak only what he hears, and he will tell you what is yet to come.

⁵⁹ Therefore go and make disciples of all nations, baptizing them in the name of the Father and of the Son and of the Holy Spirit Matt. 28:19

⁶⁰ When an impure spirit comes out of a person, it goes through arid places seeking rest and does not find it. Then it says, 'I will return to the house I left.' When it arrives, it finds the house unoccupied, swept clean and put in order. Then it goes and takes with it seven other spirits more wicked than itself, and they go in and live there. And the final condition of that person is worse than the first. That is how it will be with this wicked generation." Matt. 12:43-45

⁶¹ But others said, "These are not the sayings of a man possessed by a demon. Can a demon open the eyes of the

blind?" John 10:21

[62] But if I drive out demons by the finger of God, then the kingdom of God has come upon you. Luke 11:20

[63] For I am convinced that neither death nor life, neither angels nor demons, neither the present nor the future, nor any powers, neither height nor depth, nor anything else in all creation, will be able to separate us from the love of God that is in Christ Jesus our Lord. Rom. 8:38-39

[64] Suppose one of you has a hundred sheep and loses one of them. Doesn't he leave the ninety-nine in the open country and go after the lost sheep until he finds it? And when he finds it, he joyfully puts it on his shoulders and goes home. Then he calls his friends and neighbors together and says, 'Rejoice with me; I have found my lost sheep.' I tell you that in the same way there will be more rejoicing in heaven over one sinner who repents than over ninety-nine righteous persons who do not need to repent. Luke 15:4-7

[65] Jesus answered, "I am the way and the truth and the life. No one comes to the Father except through me." John 14:6

[66] You intended to harm me, but God intended it for good to accomplish what is now being done, the saving of many lives. Gen. 50:20

[67] In this world you will have trouble. But take heart! I have overcome the world. John 16:33

[68] For I know the plans I have for you," declares the Lord, "plans to prosper you and not to harm you, plans to give you hope and a future. Jeremiah 29:11

[69] The son said to him, 'Father, I have sinned against heaven and against you. I am no longer worthy to be called your son.' Luke 15:21

[70] For this is what the Lord says: "You were sold for nothing, and without money you will be redeemed." Isaiah 52:3

ACKNOWLEDGMENTS

You don't realize how many people support you until you decide to write a novel and everyone is cheering for you. I feel like this novel is a part of who I am, so in a way I must thank everyone who has ever spoken to me or taught me something or influenced who I am. But in particular, I must thank:

My mom. From the day we went on a quick walk that turned into a long walk while I rattled off a disjointed cluster of plot points for "this awesome new idea for a story I have," you've supported this endeavor. You've wholeheartedly encouraged me to do what I love and do it for God.

Patty. You are the most in-depth and helpful editor I've ever had the privilege to get feedback from. This story sparkles because of your insights.

Krista. In addition to being my best friend, you are my cheerleader, my sounding board, and one of the biggest reasons I became a writer at all. Your encouragement and support have kept me afloat.

Kelly, Denise, and Donna. You have been the best beta readers I could ask for. Thank you for loving on this manuscript even back when it was a bit of a mess.

My life group at church. When I get distracted from what's really important in life, you guys refocus my attention back on God. I learn so much about our creator from all of you every week.

Dad, Aaron, and the rest of my family and friends. To all of you who ask, "When is the book going to be ready?" every other day, you're all very annoying and I couldn't do it without you.

Of course, God. Thank You for all the little stories you whisper in my ear. Thank You for giving me a reason bigger than myself to do what I love. Please use me to further Your kingdom however You see fit. Please keep writing my story.

The people I've known, loved, and lost. The people I've talked to and left with a hurt in my heart that says "I must write about God and about truth, about hope and redemption and fear." I hope you find what you need.

ABOUT THE AUTHOR

Erica M Nickels has been a storyteller from the moment she first dreamed of a life beyond her own. She's addicted to playing god in universes of her own creation, taking her lead from capital-G God: the big author in the sky. Erica resides in Colorado when she's not living in a daydream.

All reviews are welcome and appreciated. Sign up for regular updates at ericamnickels.com

Made in the USA
Monee, IL
27 October 2020